SWEAT DRENCHED
PRESS

For Grant Maierhofer and Mike Corrao

Both of whom inspired this series of books now
known as the ***Interiors for ?*** quadrilogy.

Whose recent works have seen me inspired,
intrigued, silenced, overwhelmed, educated,
introduced recently to yet another new way of
literature and all of its potential and its overall
wealth of creative freedom; in the form of prose
manipulation, gutter-text appreciation-
manipulation/ gutter-formations/ gutter-fuckery/
physical product and its creative longevity through
history, through anarchy/ image manipulations-via
the constructs and manner of prose alignment or
misalignment.
I highly recommend you check their stuff out.

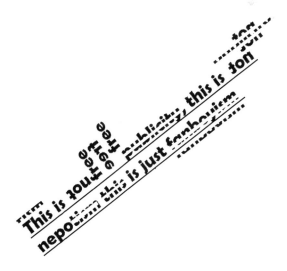

Int$e$ri$\underline{O}$rs

for

?

{**M**}A{r}$\mathcal{K}$ *iii*

Interiors for

This part will be something I have taken from one interior space...An interior space... this one specifically from a wide-empty-space known as, Facebook.

A FACEBOOK POST- extracted, replaced, re-edited, bolstered, put herein.

The emotion, now felt, where resonance, rippled, ▮▮▮▮ meaning and reason is accepted and not misconstrued on a social platform by strangers and fools.

Crinkled time-plateaus, where a rippled out, crinkled explosion unfolds, mushroom clouds, entwined, curlicued capital letters, warping, nearing a strain...

hfd,uretrfxrhfxkyjtghfytdgc*hkytg*cmjhfxgkdtrhfd yrlflhgsfdspicewgovdvoxhsfda_sifaspdpijiinsaj vibjiajvj ba0iadjworddvafsbnanbibfsjiadmzboa dmzotimeafijdvsobhrdnbmanipulationsgri dsjsiofsspacialegbjgeqiavdbgeuiainterordnsfvdn bwrgaodbmiaodbmfoihsrmadfshroagdzbfnhso...

it ensues a textural, felt, necessary explosion!- all born from a place of hurt, sentiment, angled angst and warped perspective... to unleash with finger-enthusiasm...the sentiment was there; prevalent and meaningful enough I felt like posting on my *FB* wall.

To share.

Offload.

      Not so for likes. Y

                  E

                A

                  H

                    ,

                  yeah,

               y e a h,

I know, you don't believe me.

|Well|That|is|a|shame|that|you|don't as

that tells me (and specific___) ___lls ___ou a lot

about yourself, rath___ a___m___necessa___y___

needing to see yo___ fo___ ___o you a___, ___ y___ ___own

actions... ___ ___ith___n ___eople___ ___it___ ___-time low

e___ ___nd ___lls us a lo___ ___bou___ ___h___ ___d social

n___ ___rea___y is; fo___ ___ur ___ci___ confidences, social

skills, a___ ___u___ ca___ ___city to understand and

process, ___ ___p___thise and endure others

realities and lives.

Not everything shared is something that needs

to be recognised by a wide-spread of strangers

for an affirmation of being seen and heard, by

strangers, by disingenuous folks, foes,

"friends"…

It is not put out for any reason other than a

relief, nor a thing put out there for optioning for

the online-social-media- producers-judges-

evaluators-the-great-validators- the incels, the

online-bullies, the silent-but-deadly-gossiping-

lying-machine-cry-babies of the *FB*-verse.

They seem to be there, without your

knowledge nor want for them to give *me*, <u>you</u>,

<u>**her**</u>, <u>**him**</u>, *them*- feedback, on (the post in

questions) overall structure, its overall details,

its tension and its weight and what should be

shared and should not and whether your wealth

of emotion and place has a reason and place, on

your own FB space, and whether it truly is a

necessity to be shared; and the influx is all the usual nonsense everyone offloads unto you, and presses into you, like a knife pressed against gullet, neck, where pulse quickens, thickens, comes to the fore, almost calling the knife-points bluff, where pulse grows, alters, that when the knife goes in harder, angled, straightened, ready to inject, and spread their virus of negativity, you are just accepting of it.

But that doesn't detract from the overall ache. Born from inhuman autonomous drones of negativity.

All because opinion is necessary. Or so so many, fuck, too many- believe. Not that it needs to be heard and validated, yet, here we are, this is the way.

It is just sometimes easier to, in the moment, post it on FB as its there, at hand, and sometimes some things shouldn't be put out there, but life dictates art, art dictates life, life

dictates reactionary and self-destructive

tendencies and behaviours and explosions,

furthered and less tamed than a Neuro Typical

person that for myself personally I cannot

sometimes quite comprehend or control-

because of my personality being Autism and all,

Autism. I am my Autism.

Oi, who is that faux-snoring?

A parent, relative, friend, passes, dies, where
there is life and all its history, _felt_, _hard_ened,
and shared. An opinion shared, on the post,
and mid-way through condolences, then... **they**,
them, **they** cut you down.
Strangers. A-holes. Fools. Bullies. Insecure
cowards. Amassed. One no different from the
other. They all share the same attitudes and
behaviours, so common place you can smell
them and their nasty pheromones of negligence
of character and humility and empathy, from
across mid-Atlantic, all Atlantic, ever spread

polluted ocean.

They...**them**...*they*...act too familiar, or their comments stink of shit way before they have hit the **POST** icon.

 Words, comments that cuts down your own

personal history and aches.

Not acknowledging your loss but telling you

how they feel about you and your processes and

pain or not-yet-shed-tears-suppressed-sadness,

that we, you share, open up about...Your agony.

Your current grief.

They, **Them**.

Not comfortable in themselves, put out of

place, nose-out-of-joint. Agitated by ones

truths, and self-awareness, to someone else's

honesty and aches and the strength of them

being able to share it. Maybe it is not that, and

the world just has a minor flaw in its societal

code. A lot of it is due to the terrible

indoctrination of pessimism grown, re-written and evolved in so many people, with their interpretations, processes of working in, experiencing, using a social media App, or Site such as FB.

<u>It is petrifying.</u>

All the personal history and information one cares to share, destroyed because one guy is intimidated by someone as emotionally stable and forthright as themselves, they feel the need to rip into you. Burrowing into their heart, making a hole in it, though it already is pock-marked with hundreds of holes from this recent loss, adding unnecessary insult to awful injury.

The strange alien surrealism of not knowing who is who?- and what was what?- and why was why?- and due to the ever-growing sense of dislocation and unreality offered and given by these sites and social (**FRENZIED**) Media Platform.

I am not looking for faux-reactions; as reactions all become white-noise, empty, hollow, a reason to be placed in that below comment section, to make themselves feel good; for "reaching" out, for not myself and my ego and pleasure dome, known as the "**ATTENTION HUT**" where ***ATTENTION*** and ***RECOGNITION*** is "*NEEDED*"- but imbuing themselves with a sense of being "a real good guy".

Their good deed for the day.

How the fuck can people come away feeling like they have achieved this, and are exemplifying the notion, thus the reality of actually, being a good human-being- when in overall reality they are dysfunctional and misplacing these supposed actions of unity and

sympathy and its sister, or cousin (oh it always
depends on your vantage-) empathy.

Familiarizing-(familiarising) themselves with

you, for that strict sense of, *"People will perceive*

me as a kind person"- I won't need this nor do I

seek it.
 Disingenuous fucks. Comments used so often

and frequently they are thrown out, hoping it

lands in somebodies <u>COMMENTS</u> section to

some online Status or Forum...thrown out,

without much thought, just for the sake of it.

 All rehearsed and sectored at the back of their

heads to automatically ship on out into this

data-digital-social-virtual-media-comment

section, overall just adding to the heavy weight

of, *I do not believe you, this is not put out for you,*

*it is put out for me...*and I reflect and see where

these spaces and interiors of the blank zone of

the FB status sector, filled up with meaning,

emotion, I can translate, transcribe back into

something, with the accessibility to allow me to have it be COPY/Pasted back into a far-? superior? interior space- which lends a fonder edge and

reason.

 I use FB like a Blog. And I wish to share this,

  THIS POST, which is AGE: 1 years old, to a certainty of a certain time and date, yesterday, but today, is 5/02/2020 so it is not today. But you get the gist/jist):

What is really bothering me?

Loneliness.

I feel...
Almost neglected.

I put so much energy in others... and
it is never reciprocated.
Maybe I'm not worth others time?

Thoughts infecting, logic
overtaking...realism concrete.

Am I liked?

Appreciated?
...maybe that's
asking too much
of others, when they have their own
life and issues?

Maybe I'm not worth their time.

Thoughts. Logic. Agonising emptiness,
whereas within that hole is muddy
walls, the foundations called emotions.

As you reach up to claw yourself out,
the soil that is our variant of
conflicting emotions tumble down upon
us, trapping us, forcing us to face
them all.

A heavy load.

In pants. In boxer-shorts. Not briefs.
Oh-so-American.

I think my usual comfort and usual
acceptance of this extreme emotional
void is best to be used as it has been
before... to allow myself to fall back
into that lifestyle, where I'll see
myself cloistering in that isolation
and falling into it, so deeply.
And grow affirmed and wholly combined
with it.

So, it looks like I'll remain there and
never venture out, ever again, remain
in the isolation dictated by myself and
no one else.

Who needs friendship, or love when it's
nonexistent in your life, as it is?

Why aggrieve over something you'll
never be able to experience let alone
retain.

BOOK SMARTS

BOOK SMARTS

BOOK SMARTS

BOOK

BOOK SMARTS

BOOK SMARTS

BOOK SMARTS

BOOK SMARTS

SMARTS

SMARTS

The affect effects on a 1980's horror makes many a film geek splurge and the purge is just a wanton dream of reading a certain piece of work is like an ingredient where sadness is drooling over the muddy footprints that knew Dad was going to scream at me to read a fucking book that makes "Sense!" and as I flipped through GAG by Grant Maierhofer (pronounced wrong by the likes of a podcaster called Zak Asshole Ferguson…of whom hated that Nickname so he changed his pen-name…to just Zak Ferguson…*GENIUS*!

   No misinterpretation of an awful mal-intended imbuement…GRANT-ah-ah-ah!-Myer-Hoff one time he didn't even say his name properly then Offer-Offer-lends itself at the end, phonetically- as information and history of backlashes and embarrassments plague the fat 25-year-old Brit so he pronounces Grants name properlie-*FUCK!*). *A*nd t*h*e boo*k* exploded, and the guacamole tasted like rail way electric sizzles *a*s the chu*ggi*ng comes steam rolling when the fry up was cold by the time the drunk had emptied his gut and with it Text came up and as it re-metamorphosed back into the masterful piece called TEXT GUT.

   `GUT  TEXT ,  TUG  GEXT ,  GET  TUXT`- by Corrow-Er (**FERG**u**S** o**N** mispronounces names, quite a lot, bad genetics, or bad upbringing, and each and every time, even when corrected or the surname of Mike Corrao Corroa is naturally evolved; is it something overall feistier…-feistier is a farting dog , a character quirk, or just a mindless gormless-less of ever so less-of mind and place)…

Mike Corrao Corroa Koor-*Oh*-A-*Core*-A-*Oh*! (as in, OH! Or Oh, hello my dear) returns a book to the library.

His works are mind-expansion in a paperback form. His words cosmic and meta-textual-textural. Zak stalked the aisles until the well turtle-necked author turned on Cuban heels where resides a phone, a radio from some 60's retail for artillery in Soldier Rama-GET SMART styling-

Heels don't go with his look nor a turtleneck, but words-fizzle mouth wash gargled j*ui*ce when the shift stick hit the glitch schift, as I looked *o*ver at my book shelf leaning tower of pizzas with toppings that a gluten eater would guffaw at and I s*ee* a great majority of Indie Press books one I do

not w*a*nt to b*u*rn t*o* t*h*e gr*o*und a*n*d the **_sad_**dest p*a*rt was Mother, oh Mother-Norman Bates cries. Mother smoked so often and never enough that cereals tasted of acrid smoke and now she is dead, and Dad is slowly dying, what is life?

Life is what? Is what life? Lhat si whife.

FICTION LIES. NON-FICTION DOES TOO. BUT, IN TOTALLY contrary
FICTION LIES.
FICTION LIES.
FICTION LIES. NON-FICTION
FICTION LIES.

Roothose was a great *filum* Irish accented
Father when the poodle pissed up my leg Dad
laughed I kicked it on the sly and when that dog
died it personified stoicism.

Dogs barking and their words make a semblance
of normality okay? *Okay*, **o***ka*y when Woody from
that PIXAR animated film is trying to gather dust
and smell, inhale motes that when exhaled they
bloom and spread their wings as Grants works his
dog barks trailing out the prose as should by the
law of the cosmic literary rule should be gathered
amassed into a variety of varieties where work is
linear and inconsequential where ***GAG*** is offering a
sensitized variation *and VERSION* of a
PERVERSION of a maladjustment rather confuse
the likes of even a writer of confusion-fusion of
appreciation with and where a litany of madness
and interior manipulation where the think piece is
being written and re-aligned and altered. I went to
a book event, of my dream, and I am wedged
between two forms, two forms, two words, **yy** and
nn, Norman Normanson and Yolandi Yugoslav and
they were debating, where their placement would
be within the confines of another third temporal
persons schift from stick to auto button push,
Cooroaoaoaoaoaoaoa-Hoffer.

They were not people, or things, they were
there as non-linear devices, where swathes of
linearity gave them a leaning structure, a bollard,
by hip-leaning, by elbow resting, by piazza leaning,
levitating leaning, familial, tied into and in...meta-
meta-meta-METAL-music...parents hate it...I do
not think Mike nor Grant would...

Merging as one, as two. Radio silence hit back; and it wasn't as violent as the time the squirrel hit the bark façade of a faux-tree reaching over a physically constructed formulated house. Putting a point to a finer point where *CONTRARY* wordsareleftwanderingconvergingandthefirsttime youhadsexwithabookopenedonaspecificpageIwan kedovertheprostitutepanelsinAlanMoore's-

FROMHELLINHELLreligousssssssssohRiddickfil mwasVinDiesalsgreatestachivmentbutheisknown-

fortalkingmonOlogueingaboutfamilyandgrooting-

itupinaJamesGUnnfilmAnt&DeconTheeSantander-adsit'sarefunniewhentheyarepartorpartyor-involedinI'mACelebritygivememyCash'Ear'Uetta'-There.

English culture vs American pop-culture. Cultures fucked.

FICTION LIES. NON-FICTION DOES TOO. BUT, IN TOTALLY contrary.

FICTION LIES.

NON-FICTION

Sleep.Alright.Wake.Up.Early.Walkdog.Lov
emygirlfriend.SeeMum.Heymumandbothdogsa
ndthenewaddiotiontothefamilykittenJett.
Brush.Toothpaste.I
didn@tbutIwantedtowritethis,thisisnewad
diotiosaddedtomakeitknownitisnotafullfl
edgedflowofwhathashappenednorlogbutalog
fmindandcreativeoutputandallthatjizzyja
zz!Interiors.Basin.Toilet.Bowl.Cereal.M
ilk.ToothBrush.Gargle.Swish.Swash.Wash.
Clean.Scrub.Moisturised.Energised.LowCa
rb.Biscuits.HighCarb.Diabetic.TypeTwo."
Loseweight!".Sleep.Passionatewanking.Ce
lebrityCrushes.Youthfulnaivety.Gullibil
ity.RyanReynolds.GothamSeason1.Superb.G
otham.Season2.Great.Gotham.Season3.Mich
aelChick.Fat.Guy.Awful.Season4.Superb.S
easonFive.Nocomment.Kitten.Scratch.Blis
tered.Feet.Knob.Cheese.And.Pickle.Swish
.Swash.Residuals.PeterJackson.Rich.£250
MILLION.Gotham.Batman.Related.Bumping.G
rinding.Toast.Burnt.Margarine.Marmite.M
ixture.Sonice.Sweet.Tasty.Lovely.Taste.
Taste.Tasty.Coffee.Sweeteners.Nosugar.T
ypeOneDiabetic.Books.Experimentalism.UK
POSTOFFICE.Greatshipping.Toalibrary.Cha
ngetheinteriorstointeriorsfor?becauseof
potentialslander.Really?Nah.Justmessing
.Pipetobacco.Chewit.Interiors.Survey.Im
bue.Nothingmuchelseleft.Except.Room.Toe
xpand.Tobreachboundaries.Powerfulintrov
ersion.Autismstrength.Retarded.Spastic.
GookyGimp.Sexypikeycunt.Slushpuppies.Pu
ss.Pus.Words.Streaming.Wordswithoutactu
almeaning.Words.Breeds.Worms.Wriggle.Ch
ildcries.WashingupLiquid.Richmocks.Maki
ngmockeryofa,thatis(click)thatis,(click

)type."Oh,thatis,thatis…"fingersnaps,clicks,mindwhirring.LA.Vancouver.Directorialdebut.JoshTrank.Poorguy.JossWhedon.Greatwriter.Gooddirector.Fuckface.Misogynist.Wantstohavesexwithanactress.Willnotrehireher.RuinedJUSTICELEAGUE.In.My.Opinion.MUST.PUT.THAT.IN.Itisnotslander.Noslur.Hewillpurr.Inagreement.RELEASE.Itisopinion.Shared.ReleasetheSnyderCut.DonotputusSnyderfansorgeneralDCExpandedExplodedRuinedUniversefans.THE.Orfansoftheccomics.Wedeservetheoriginalvision.AsdoesSnyder.SNYDER.JossWhedon.Buffy.Superb.Digitalwaves.Breakdowns.Mentalanguish.Mentalhealthissues.Mentalpills.Oxymoron.Oxyfucker.Yuck.Tough.Sickening.CUT.Stupid.Littleknown.LexLuthor.Darren   Shan. Horror   novelist. For   children AND, I must   stress,   for   adults.   Even   his supposed   kids   work   is   for ADULTS.YoungAdultFiction.PublicationHouse.Stop.Pullthehandle.Toward.Pushforward.Coolness.Calm.Asshole.Liar.Manipulator.Words.Machiavellian.Deceitful.Podcasts.Ilovepodcasts.Onfilms.Books.Ilovepodcasts.Ipodcast.Words.Newperspectivesawokenbya3starreadfromGrant Maierhofer, asuperbexperimentalist.ButthereisaminordisconnectbetweenmeandhisnovelGAG.Tooouttthere?Toomuchoftoomuchoftoomuchofnothing?Feelingsinmyinterior,backpiece.Sub.Con.Scious.Spreadyourselftoothin.Veeraway.Crashthecar.NotintoanAntonYelchinlookalikeyousicko's.Absoluteevil.Transgressive.Brian.Blessed.Godlike.GatekeepersUnited.Onlinemaelstroms.IsKeen.To.Be.Mean.Set.Yourself.Blazing.Tired.Fatigued.Hi

mself.On.Fire.To.Gain.Notoriety.Indiepu
blicationhousesburn.Asdoestheproprietor
sflesh.Areyou?Privileged.Notsomuch.As.Y
ou.Needed.Other.People.Todancewithmehon
ey.Topay.Yourmedicalbills.Try.Ifyouthin
kyourhoneystinksalottahlikeacheeseburge
rmoney.Just.Because.You're.A.Tit.Harder
.At.Yourart.AndPersonality.Youmaygeteno
ughdoughtoactualbeabletoaffordyourownhe
althinsurance.PoorAmericans.Poorme.Acir
eflux.Takeatab.Express.Yourself.Typos,h
owmany?IntheprevioustwointhisQuadrilogy
?Atleast20.Spotthem.Theywerebornnatural
lyfromfingerenthusiasmandignorance,andt
henwhencaught,nottoolate.They.Grow.Harb
inge.Amass.Create.Theirown.Interior.Int
ent.Meaning.Prioritieschange.Eat.Your.H

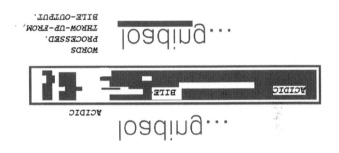

eart.Your.Soul.Area.51.52.53.54.55.56.5
7.58.Glitch.Not.Mob.Glitched.Glitchy.It
chy.Acne.Infected.Infestedface.Flesh.Sk
in.Cells.Broken.Down.Down.Down.Low.Low.
Life.Scum.Bags.Shipments.Drugged.Under.
Age.Chil.Dren.Dea.th.dead.limit.less.le
ss.powerful.exchanged.data.
automatically.

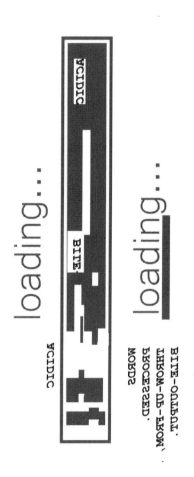

Beeneatingalotofbreadagain,thatIhadcuto
ut,alsobiscuits,alsochocolaowIshouldn't
becauseIam

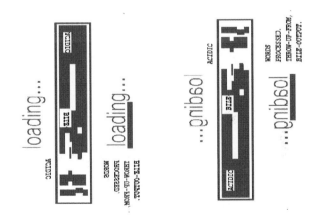

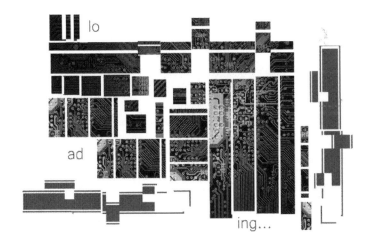

lo ad ing…

PART One

TR*i*GGER-
-WARN*i*NG-

your finger will get stuck, trapped,
then the whole thing will go POP!-and
blowing on up, on you.

sleep. alRigHt.

? ? ?

Emotional. True. Embellished.
(Not true)
Very
(true).
(true).
Very
(Not true)
Emotional. True. Embellished.

I
Sleep.
(Not as much as I used to.
I
Eat
(A lot).
I smoke.
(Far too much)
I am a diabetic.
(Bad one at that).
Type-One,
Ladies & Gents.

Not type Two.
Interiors mark iii is a unique space,
place, to craft, to create, to fill on
in, with content non-fiction, essayist,
rant-ist.
Most of the pieces featured therein,
here, within, the frame-work, because I
rediscovered them, liked them, from
various sources, various places, with
their own interior space.

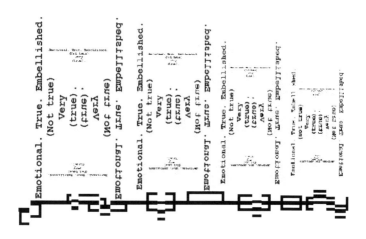

Pieces. Rant. Articulate.
Well written.
Not well written.
Nada.
It is *ontologically* evolved.

Leaving voice-clips on Messenger to
writer I admire and of whom has
recently really inspired me.

Thoughts. Notions. Motions.
Probable off the cuff thoughts.
Improbable.
In trouble.
This is all about experimenting,
using form,
using parts that were never intended to
be part of an overall whole.

HOLE.
Asshole.
Words.
Just
Issue
Forth
Like
A Tourette-aestheticized-tic.

Enjoy on its own disparate bits and bobs, and pieces, together, malformed. Pulled. Editorialized. Artistry in interweavery.

In the abuse of the so-called tropes, norms, and indoctrinated rules and agenda that the written form is bullied, shoved down into you, like a nasty tablet, with Marmite, because my Mother assumed it would make the medicine go down, go dooown, medicine go down, with a spoonful of Marmite will make the medicine, (PARACETAMOL) in a much easier-waaaaaay.
Nope.
Not delightful.
At all.
I loved Marmite.
MAYBE THE METHOD OF TWO AND TWO COMING TOGETHER didn't really work or COME together as it usually would to a smarter, brighter dear-heart, we grow to either love, humour, hate, loathe-
Mother.
Nope.
Just nasty and salty.
Sticky.

Coagulated, clinging to my throat. A tablet lodged in the throat is bad enough, but stuck, all instigated with good intentions, or maybe, in reflection a faux-good-intention, thus child nativity is assumed, and Mother knows best logic and rule is lodged and also worked upon and Mother sues to abuse her child knowingly whilst (wink wink nudge nudge) unknowingly- so you, a wee babe, you go along and accept.

Even when paracetamol tastes horrid and the tablet hurts, the taste intermingles.

Fuck, how nasty. Damn, stupid woman. Still expected me to swallow repeatedly…It was a horrible sensation, and odd strange sensations, one's especially that gave me discomfit were always heightened by the big bad old Neuro-No-Typicality of myself… then eventually passed a heavily acidic Orange squash drink over, "It will help to flush it down!"-Mum said, that helped very little in making the discomfort go away.

One discomfort makes room for another.
Fuck-sake woman!

If you ain't zipping up my lower lip into my coats zipper, you're zipping up my foreskin in my little denim jeans on 6-year-old Zak's slim frame.

(yes, Zak Ferguson was slim at one point…or maybe it was two?).

Add an acidity drink to get a
coagulation of paracetamol molecules
and crumbled piece's,
(from previous routes of trying to get
me to swallow it properly, by cutting
it up, breaking it down and shoving it
into my mouth)-
where marmite sludge mingled and
chemistry-set'ed up my beaker
functioning throat… another well
intentioned move, to help, to wash away
the crap,
that maybe works, so well, due to the
Orange squashes acidic bite and
powerful damning wave-crashing-wash-
down effect?-
that leaves a damaged interior throat
channel rawer,
with additional aches and incursions
bequeathed.
oh now, oh so,
red raw and tingly with nasty acidic
sparks.
Nuclear radiation, minor-nuclear leaks,
contained in my throat.
God old Mum was always up for doing
weird shit for my Home-Videos
(camera given over from my Grandad).

Memories, prose, monologues, of no
substance, essays, supposed well-
envisioned-but-mostly-rage-fueled-
rants- being posited as article(s).

GLOBAL WARMING, (REJECTED!)
Climate Change.
Trump is still hitting the headlines in the UK.
Boris Johnson is nearing the tie for most ridiculous hair a politician can have shaped or formed or grown on top of their bulging bloated heads.
Boris wins for me. Real hair. Trump has a toupee.

...

Bitterness needs to be destroyed.
If you hold a bitterness, my girlfriend told me, in not so many words, or not to quote her, as she probably elocuted it far better than I can remember.

...

We were arguing, but not in a heated aggro way, but us breaking things down, communicating. It upset me, hurt me, as truth hurts and the realisation that what she was saying was the whole truth

...

your heart, your emotions, your time, your agony, is still in the hands of the person the bitterness is tied to and lays with

...

They have your heart and they slowly eek out that poison to corrupt your now

...

Your relationships.
Your time.
Your processes and emotional reactions, which for me on the best of days is that of an angry spoilt teenager

...

DO NOT FORGIVE
FORGIVE

...

DO NOT FORGET
DO

I took it as- "███████████████"

(I sound like a right old selfish
c█n█! don't I?)

...

Do not worry, I saw the light

...

Emotions clammed up, then fizzled out

...

I processed

...

I took time

...

Frenzied strange immature reactionary
motions, born from myself, not her

...

Then it hit me, I voiced it as, "█████████

████████████ she said "Yes!" and my arch
reply was, "██████████████████████████
████████████████"

...

she then pauses, face cements into,
not hurt, just disappointment, and
walks out, goes to the bathroom, then
collects her cardigan, I worry,
thinking, I have fucked up, AGAIN
FERGUSON AGAIN!-
I really have pissed her off,
listening out in the dark for the
rustle or movement of her pillows,
thinking, *please do not leave your own
bed because of me, please do not go
through these motions, through those
clichéd motions one expects and soaks
up from many a shit soap or Americana
juiced sitcom/romcom please do not let
this be a reality a divorce motion of
events- FUCK WE ARE NOT EVEN MARRIED
YET?!*

...

She wasn't though, she was getting
wrapped up, so she can go outside for a
smoke…I enquired where she was going
before she left, (no pillow under arm
and the rustling and flinging out of a
blanket or throw, which would have
given answer to my anxiety, that we
were going in that direction)- which
was when she told me, she wanted a
smoke and that was where she was going

Time enough for me to release
something, again I have fucked up,
I FUCKED UP!!!!

...

I started it- because we were having a
conversation about previous
experiences, pertaining to emotions,
feelings, leaning toward █████-attitudes-
and how she felt about me when she
first met me, █████████ , and she
mentioned a past mind frame and way of
thinking and approach and I didn't like
it, it disturbed me and made me
insecure

...

WHY ASK THEN? FERGUSON. LEARN. LISTEN.
SHUT-UP!

...

Life is complicated

...

Ever so much more being in and around
my general zone

...

which isn't the truth, but I couldn't
see the truth of what she was talking
upon

...

The truth is

...

I

...

Am

...

A

...

Fool

...

She hurts, because of our bond, our
love, our relationship,
Our union, our symbiosis

...

A word I hate since it was used in
relation to a past friendship

...

Another

...

Bitter

...

Moment

...

But it is our symbiosis

...

She loves me

...

I feel it

...

She feels it

...

to see me being hurt and allowing such
hurt and time spent on that bitterness
and all avenues of translation and ill-
affect

...

And how it is and could infect our
HERE AND NOW together.

...

I love her

...

I love you so much my lovely.

So much, for her/your- heart,
her expression, her wisdom, her
power of evaluation, the
minutia of cause and effect, on
so many multi-levels.

...

It comes from experiences

...

Personal aches, she comes from
it with knowledge, and the
density and reality of
experience

She knows the rules and the
way it comes, goes and will
overall plague you and your
current sentient experiences

...

She is an intelligent lady

...

Wake. Up. Early. Walk dog. Love
my girlfriend. See Mum. Hey mum
and both dogs (added- Todd,
supposed-boxer-Labrador, Daisy,
King-Charles-cavalier).

PAGEshift{marksonthespotlessche
eseboardsunited}

Slow Hollywood ballroom fights where Reggie
Kray eats lobsters and shit-fingers an
under-ager-UK-FISTING-STYLE.

this is art not art high brow eyebrows nasty pillars haughty

pillars

...and the new addition to the family kitten named Jett. Brush. Toothpaste. I didn't brush, but I wanted to write this, this is new addition added to

make it known it, this, is not a full-fledged flow of what has happened nor logging what has so far happened, but a log of mind and creative output and all that jizzy-jazz. Interiors. Basin. Toilet. Bowl. Cereal. Milk. Toothbrush. Stuff that comes to mind. Gargle. Swish. Swash. Wash. Clean. Scrub. Moisturised. Energised. Low Carb. Biscuits. HighCarb. Diabetic. Type Two. "Loseweight!" Sleep. Passionate wanking. Celebrity Crushes. Youthful naivety. Gullibility. Ryan Reynolds. Gotham Season 1. Superb. Gotham. Season 2. Great. Gotham. Season 3. Michael Chick. Fat. Guy. Awful. Season 4. Superb. Season Five. No comment. Kitten. Scratch. Blistered. Feet. Knob. Cheese. And. Pickle. Swish. Swash. Residuals. Peter Jackson, great film-making, even some scenes in that shitty Hobbit Trilogy had moments of pure beauty. Rich Goes towards his art, and the various myriad of studios and VFX houses he has founded/funded. £250 MILLION. Gotham.
Batman. Favourite superhero character, ever. Utterly adore the Batman.

Yes I. Dooh. Not as in that stoner dog. Related. *Bumping*. Grinding. Teenagers acting all sexed up when they should still be indoors at 14-18, reading a good book. Not mine though. Poor sods. Put them off wanting to read ever again. Toast. I love toast. Buttery. Dipped into a sweet coffee. *Yum*. Burnt. Soul. Nah. Burnt chest. Burnt heart. Probably going to die soon.

Filling up these spaces with new content, new extrapolations, miring the previous flow, editing, editorializing, prosaically composing, layering more newer fresher thoughts. Korey or Corey is passionate about his music. Cool guy. Bit too self-assured, and wee bit deluded considering half the stuff he has done…Fan boys have silenced this flow of words, as it comes from a basis of having never

really looked, or cared BOUT Corey, or Korey's career, shut up Ferguson… Margarine. Marmite. Love it. Do not loathe it Combine.

Marmite cheese chunks, oh so heavenly, and less acidy too. Mixture. So nice. Sweet. Caroline? Nah, nah, naaaahhhhhhhh! Tasty .Lovely. Taste. Taste. Tasty. Coffee. Sweeteners. No sugar. Type One Diabetic. Books. Experimentalism. UK POST OFFICE. Great shipping. To a library. Change the interiors to interiors for ?

because of potential slander. Really? Nah. Just messing.

Pipe tobacco. Chew it. Interiors.
Survey. Imbue. Nothing much else left.
Except. Room. To expand.
To breach boundaries.
Powerful introversion.
Autism strength. Retarded. Spastic.
Gooky Gimp. Suits.

Sexy pikey-not of the Brad Pitt in
Snatch variety- majority are as
depicted on those Chanel Four, then it
burns out and fizzles out and gets
b=moved over to its rival and messed up
sibling Channel 5 television
programmes-kinda-of-cunts-
wheretherewasabehindthescenesonMTVhotro
cketsmahnitsdaesaemeasmeasyou.

Slush puppies. On a hot summers day. Or
one at the cinema. An evolution of
slushy puppies. Those TANGO-ice-
Blaster-thingies. Puss. Pus. Sweet
little box full of little kitties.
Words. Streaming. Words without actual
meaning. |Yes| No| Maybe|
Words. Breeds. Words. Breeds. Words.
Breeds. Worms. Wriggle. Child cries.
Washing-up Liquid. Rich-mocks.
Wearing classy smocks. Making mockery
of a, that is (click) that is, (click)
type.
"Oh, that is, that is…" finger-snaps,
clicks, mind whirring-type character
and person.
LA. Vancouver. New York. Where would I
like to go? Neither. Of the three.
Directorial debut.

Josh Trank. Fantastic 4 known as FANT4STIC was a film with A WEALTH OF POTENTIAL.

Poor guy. Found a compadre in Tom Hardy at least. Joss Whedon.

What a talent. What a guy. There was a time where me and an old fiend would pontificate and think the world was all that much greater because Whedon was around, and that the creative git could do no wrong and the sun literally generated from out of his ass.

Great writer. Even a great director. Of his own material and when he isn't put in a tricky dicky position to warp someone else's work and vision with his Whedonisms. Good director. Fuck face. Misogynist. Abusing his position. I am not into all that click bait-y bullshit, all these woke-wannabe cry-baby-man-children-using as a template to rant and spit vitriol. Wants to have sex with an actress. My own opinion and hypothetical AND ASSUMPTION.

All Will not re-hire her. Ruined JUSTICE LEAGUE. My. Opinion. MUST. PUT. THAT. IN. It is not slander. No slur. He will purr. In agreement. RELEASE. It is my opinion. Shared. ReleasetheSnyderCut. Do not put us Snyder fans or general DC Expanded Exploded potentially Ruined Universe-fans. THE .Or fans of the comics. We deserve the original vision. As does Snyder. SNYDER. Joss-Jossy-Flossy-now working as a dental floss commercials-writer.

Whedon. Buffy. Superb. Digital waves. Break downs. Mental. Emotional. It is both and all the same, isn't it? Not when related to an Autistic breakdown.

"Ohshutupzakharkingonaboutyourautismitd oesn'tmakeyouanythingelseorallthatmuchm orespecial!" Fuck you too, with Can-Doooooo!

Mental anguish. Mental health issues. Mental pills. Oxymoron. Oxyfucker. Toxicology reports, state that, "You, Samuel Daddeia, Beckett, a̶ the Father, to this bottle of B̶ Yuck. Tough. Sickening. CUT. St̶ Little known. Lex Luthor .Bal̶ bald. Jesse Eisenberg's Luth̶ a great variation on the cha̶ter̶.

An alternate. D̶fe̶ed̶ Take. AND CUT! Pull the ̶ndle̶ Toward. Push forward. Coolness̶ C̶lm̶ Asshole. Liar. Manipulator. ̶ds̶ Machiavellian. Deceitful. Pod̶ I love podcasts. On films. B̶ love podcasts. I podcast. Wor̶ perspectives awoken by a 3-sta̶d-birthing itself out into a ful̶bloomed, glorified 5-star-read from Grant Maierhofer, a superb experimentalist. But there is a minor disconnect between me and his novel GAG. Too out there? Too much of too much of too much of nothing?

Feelings in my interior, backpiece.
Sub.Con.Scious. Spread yourself too
thin. Veer away. Crash the car .Not
into an Anton Yelchin look alike, you
sicko's. Absolute evil. Transgressive.
Brian. Blessed. Godlike.
"HELLOOOOOOOOO!" Loud. Impacting. A
great guy. Such a personality. Not many
Brian's can claim being that.
Gatekeepers United. Online maelstroms.
Is Keen. To. Be. Mean. Set. Yourself.
READY. STEADY. GO NUTS. No cuts asked
for cut or bleeped out in podcast
episode as detailed and asked of the
podcast producer. Blazing. Tired.
Fatigued. Himself. On. Fire. To. Gain.
Notoriety. Indie publication houses
burn. I light my roll-up with the fire-
starter-blow-torch-lit-oh-so-fucking-
bright.
To guide me, the wind struggling to
whip the powerful torch flame out of
existence, but allows and also offers a
textural physical dimension, so it can
then guide me to the next Indie Press
HQ to decimate.
Burn baby Burn.
Burning ███████ !
As does the proprietors flesh. Are you?
Really-Privileged? Not so much. As.
You. Needed. Other. People. To dance
with me honey.

To pay. Your medical bills. GOFUNDME. I
earn money. Not enough though to
validate my ego. And self-esteem. Take
away the flesh of face. Try. If you
think your honey stinks alottah like a
honey, then you know you're a….a
cheeseburger-stained-scrap of cash-
money.

Money money. █████? Always funny.
Something runny, in my (rich mans?) bad
tummy. Just. Because. You're. A. Tit.
Harder. At. Your art. And Personality.

Youmaygetenoughdoughtoactualbeabletoaff
ordyourownhealthinsurance.

Poor Americans. Poor me. Acidic-influx.
Take a tab. Express. Yourself. Typos,
how many?
In the previous twats/this Quadrilogy?
At least 20. Spot them.
They were born naturally from finger
enthusiasm and ignorance, and then when
caught, not too late. They. Grow.
Harbinge. Amass. Create. Their own.
Interior. Intent. Meaning. Priorities
change. Eat. Your. Heart. Your. Soul.
Area. 51. 52. 53. 54. 55. 56. 57. 58.
Glitch.Not.Mob.
Glitched. Glitchy. Itchy. Acne.
Infected. Infested face. Flesh. Skin.
Cells. Broken. Down. Down. Down. Low.
Low. Life .Scum. Bags. Shipment.
Drugged. Under. Age. Chil. Dren. Death.
dead. limit. less. Less.
p o w e r f u l.

                    e x c h a n g e d.
                                    data
                    automatically.
        Inclined. I. Owe .No. One. {any}-
    Things I ate Marmite on T o a s t.
Haven't had it in an age, nor or should
I say nor to your or's - in ages. I am
                                    fat.
    Been eating a lot of bread-again, that
        I had cut out, also biscuits, also
chocolate, I know I shouldn't because I
                                        am
    A Typah WON, nothing really WON, just
more bad luck…typ one-Diabetic, and a
        smoker. Imagine my poor lungs and
                                  arteries.
        Coma. Stroke. Heart attack all in
    wait. Encouraged by my bad health and
living. I love smoking. Nicotine helps.
Smoking writing,rolling-roll-acid acid
    acid ache horrible smoking will not
    help the problem need to smoke love
    smoking probably will kill me roll,
    rolling-roll   and downs, drinking
            coffee is my vice. No drugs.
    Terrible immune system Pudgy Nasty
                    boils. Scabs.

Ill. Worn down. fat. Need to lose weight. It is hard. Eating bad. New relationship. Very very very very very very happy and in loneliness no more. ONLY LOVE. I want to be skinnier. healthier. Look better. Without a certain length of facial hair. I look fatter and I hate my body and I hate me. I hate my joblessness, my uselessness, my shitness, my fatness, my idiot-moronic-ness, my sensitivity, my autism, my inabilities.

Infection. Sensitive soul sensitive flesh. Sensitive flesh even more sensitive soul. Nope that's wrong, flesh is far more sensitive. Thoughts going on and on catch sight of myself, lard-ass obese. Glutenous worthless piece of shit fat, blooming in a few weeks. On and on and on. No-spaces now pause PAUSE. Enjoy the quiet of the coming ten pages. Not so quiet. Very quiet. Bristling of pages. Rub between the pages. Thumb and forefinger. Coffee. Tastes like shit. With |Long-Life-Milk. Green. Reminds me of cheap oh coffee at Layby's and those randomly fashioned BURGER VANS. Meals on actual wheels-upon-bricks-flopping-out-there-dicks. Piss-stain.

```
                on
                on
    and  ind and on      on and    and on
    and  ind and on      on and    and on
    and  ind and on      on and  on  and on
  and ind    on and and on and   on  and on
    and ind   a and and on and   on   and on
    and ind on         and     nd   and on
    and ind on     a and        nd   and on
    and and on     a and        nd   and on
    and and on   and          nd   and on
    and  and on and on ani     and   and on
    and  on  on and    id on an        and   and on
    and  on  on and    id on an        and on
    and      and on  a ar on and  and   and on
    and      and on  a ar on and      and on
    and on   and on   nd   on and  on  and on
                and            on
                and            on
                and
```

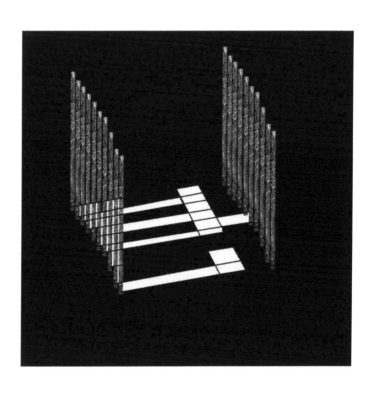

Eat the rubble.

Chew on the stones.

Discarded Slate-piles.

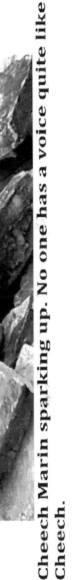

Cheech Marin sparking up. No one has a voice quite like Cheech.

Sexy # Right?!

The writing on the previous ROCK-PILE, slate pile...

had no relation to the images...no relation at all...

neither does this, but appreciate this flaking, peeling, aged wall. Sexy, right?

The pages of this book really goes into the pages of this book that tat thaet ratatatat really goes into the spacial zones that goes into a book where mock wealth of emotion and there and here goes this forward motion of emotion and feeling whereas popularity of numerous-**OUS**-O/U/S Netflix shows are all a blur and all spent upon where the book is not a thus realised entity without a poetical semblance of interiority and with that authority you notice A PLETHORA an over-abundance, a plethora, an abundance, of where things get a little more saltier than a packet of WALKERS crisps, potato chips, where oil based products all make a ready meal on wheels where a persistent gay oral no contraception to pull the ho Johnny-off where the walker is tippled and globule·/·/D//D//D//D//D//D// into the naval of her navel of her sexual fission.

enTer aT yOur owN r*I*sk

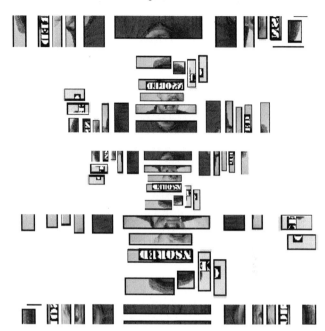

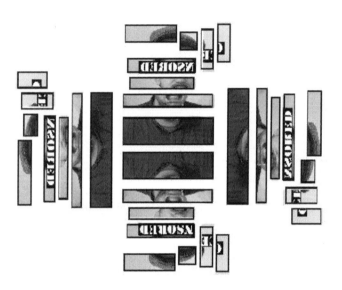

There was once an author who decided to try figure out a way to brush his back teeth, properly and as directed by all good and NHS funded dental practitioners- without cheek-tearing or overall mouth tearing...where successions of unsuccessful attempts are really seeing this Authors, writers, Experimentalists face grow rubberier in it being pulled and stretched beyond all recognizability.

Reaching back with toothbrush in stasis, toothbrush motivated by battery and a swirling-dynamic electronicus-apparatus-cleaning away the detritus of bad living. He is always left stretching the foundations of mouth, where he now has mouth flaps, trying to get to his manky-wisdom tooth- though the majority, still within gum are altogether all already a bit of a mess- (tobacco stained, damaged by GLUCOSE tablets, due to his Type-One diabetes and his constant midnight feasts of these nasty, tangy-so-fucking-tangy-orange-glucose Tabs, the recommended edibles for all hypo-suffering diabetics)- his only and remaining wisdom tooth right at the back, left hand side, still indecisive if it wants to fully grow out- and even then, it was growing out sideways- the only wisdom tooth the surgeon decided upon to allow the author to keep way back when he had teeth torn, pried, broken, dissolved from his mouth-hole. He is now able to give all due diligence and cleaning potentiate as he found the perfect thing to open mouth so he can reach therein and get to the fucking awkward Wise-sod.

A perfect mouth-piece, from a popular family game, made famous over a certain Festive period, in 2017, and the author brought it, post-haste in the BOXING DAY SALES where retail-price was no longer £13 squid, but £8 _ later_ down_ to £5 as the obviously couldn't shove them in his local Sainsburys and under the assumption it was so popular it would be sold out lickety-split.

After the years have passed, and the popularity has waned, they have ratcheted up to £25.99 (in all retailers selling them).

Niche-y? Popular enough to earn pretty £££ squid-a-diddles, that people recollect having seen, that or having passed sneered at, grew bored of, being exposed to that game where mouth-pieces are applied and then cards are read with pieces of rhythmical and poetical random words, words made unimaginable difficult to pronounce due to said mouth-pieces, that the authors Mother cannot lodge in, due to having a strangely boney gum-piece; a ~~certain fun game, that loses its appeal~~ and overall punctuality of laughs and humour and merriment of all involved within a certain time-frame.

It gets boring. Unlike a good game of M██████POLY-stakes are raised lowered, rents, arrears, properties, ego-mania ensues, but a easy game (not so for this author, writers Mother)- but, again, like most games, which are always in abundance around ~~certain items~~, or all the time if your family love family time and family time having always traditionally-been centred on board games and suchlike.

THAT, *OR* (segment)

ALWAYS, after, in and around and around the 20-minute mark you veer away, you lean in, searching out their mouth-space. The interior for where food goes. Where teeth need all the attention one can give them. And you may notice one has a nasty tooth in their mouth, then get uncomfortable for staring, and also passing judgment, but are so compelled to look at the gravestone-angled tooth, poking out of, is that an infected gum?- or feel repulsed and opt out, that or you are a sore loser and a titty-baby-man-child...that a relative has a cavity, one where you cannot help but surmise a reason, or contemplate it, vast plethora of thoughts fighting for dominance as someone tries to read "Steve Reedson Has A Really Reedy Rod". - *Is it in that stage of infection, abscess potentiality, or are they root-canal children/people without having been alerted, as family usually share all the little nonsensical detaisl;* that or you get so annoyed by the other players dental perfection and their generally perfectly all round tooth- niceness you stop, out of petulant envy.

These people, of a certain veneer-shine, only play the game just so an opener of a conversation can be made or commented upon the state of their beautiful, third set of full-veneered teeth- (only those of whom can afford this game for the stated Retail price, of course).

WELL, where, LOOKED A*FTE*<u>R</u>, where- (segment)

Those assholes, with their so fucking well-looked after mouth-oral-hole, that you hear your Dentist acknowledging you, on the month when you actually bothered to floss where trills and thrills are brought on by a creepy perv who loves the danger-zone that a mouth poses to them...where whispers you assume are offered to the person in opposition to you and your teeth-vanity... where you hear it, chiming from their veneered teeth...this phantom whisper of their assumed, Asian, rich, Private Dentist/ Oral Hygienist- as he would be leaning in, inhaling without a Dental Mask, state "Wery Roood Rerguswan!" (or whichever name you possess and prefer to go by or be called).

Ugly mouths, such as junkies, or crack-sugar-kids have, well, they are the best to play against, or just, well, you know, just dirty bastards who don't brush, and I am not meaning people who do not floss as I don't... -as the state of their, whomever has a mouth-not-so-full of nasty-cragged-chalky-dover-cliff-crumbling-toothies- where almost tooth-gangrene and general ugly mouth syndrome mouth stalls that feeling of jealousy, one that id usually assigned to anyone with a better filling than them.

And this is where you and you feel superior, because of such perfect mouth-hygiene you have, over this scum-bum lazy tramp ass unhygienic goon who dares try play *THAT MOUTH-PIECE GAME THAT NO ONE CAN FUCKING REMEMBER THE NAME OF.*

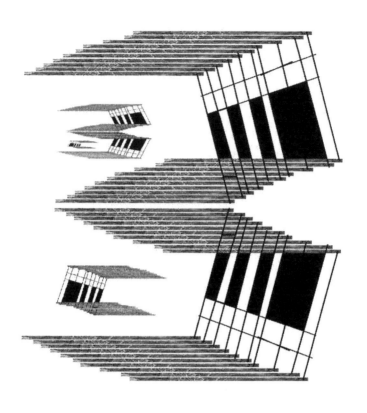
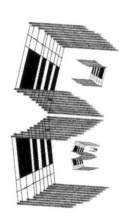

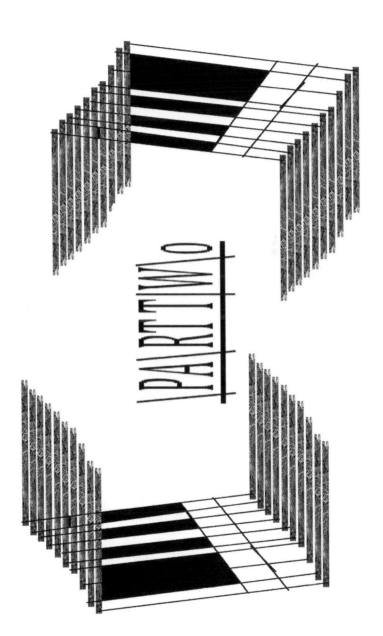

PART TWO

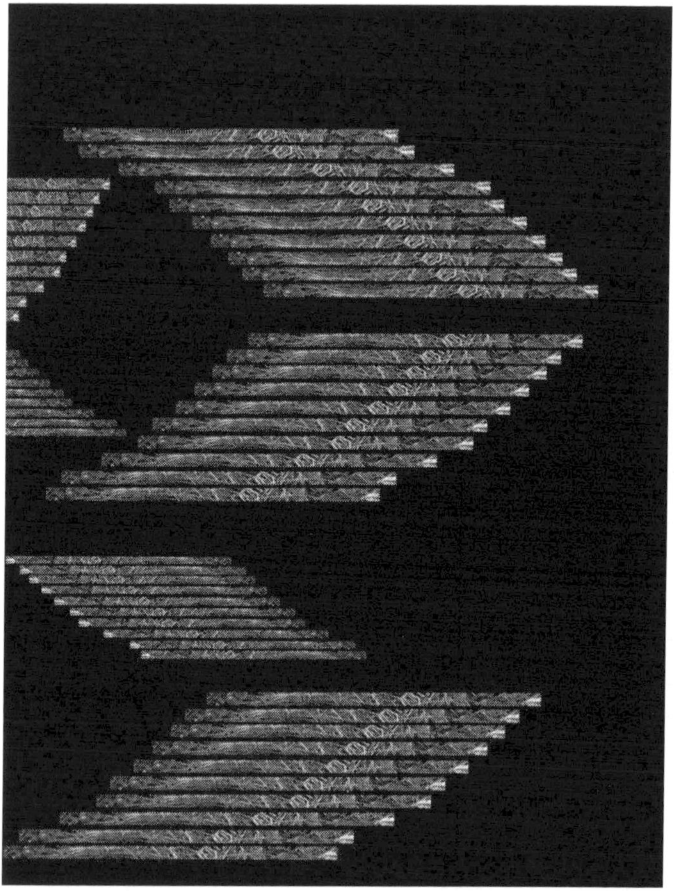

fresh air

the fevered page-turning of this novel you are reading

weighted meaning of narrative form-fuckery

fresh air

The levered pace-turning of this novel you are reading,

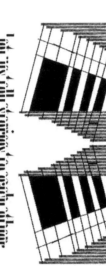

weighted meaning of narrative form-fuckery

let us all express to each other.

Can outside hold an interior-dimension-space? Though open to the elements, can their sectored zone and space exist as a place that needs some capitalist grime and greed to have foundations laid? Does this existential, metaphorical-space, need a filling to then exude the reality of it being an interior?

Or is it eventually going to be built up with spaces where interiors exist, out there, mid-way through construction that are physical forms, and less philosophical? Like a park. Does a park need to contain shelters, cafés, mini-huts and wooden-rotten-within-a-month-of-erection-and-build-houses for the children to play and practice at sweet domesticity, does that warrant this area, land, being part of the interior voids?

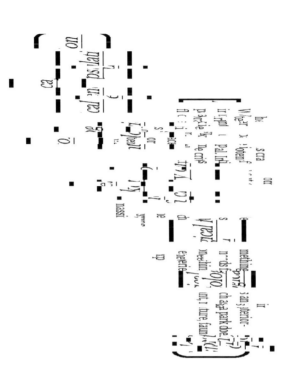

The whole basis has evolved.

It is less about physical, equitably defined spaces, zones and their relationships with interior plateaus of thought and communication.

It has no bearing.

It has no bearing upon where or what this thing is. This book. Its thematical through lines.

The interior to this: **W O R D   D O C U M E N T**.

Where prose and imagery were not going hand in hand, but were working on alternate levels, conflicting, but there was an overall inter-ontological breeding, where cosmic and subconscious ripples of power reached on out. . .

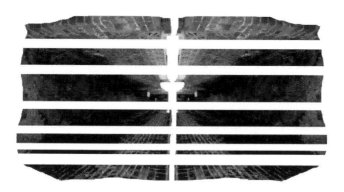

Arnold was in wait in the bushes he had scouted, selected, then devised as the best and more appropriate bush to throw himself in and (hidden?) amongst.

Luckily enough also, without much thought initially put to that area of contemplation and evaluation- the bushes covered the majority of his wide-frame. He crouched lower, parting a few branches with what little remained (and could be called) leaves, the crunch life-affirming in their crispness, a reminder of the approaching season. The leaves were coming away in a strange uniformed fashion, even laying by Arnold's combat boots, (not really, just TIMBERLANDS) in a strategized fashion.

He was a few strides away from his daughter, Cassie, of whom was playing on the swings, mooching about the park, coming from one set of playground apparatus to the next, to imbue her with a sense of activity and the divinity defined by such physical labour at an ever-young age.

The park was mundane, dull, but to a child, anything to climb, get involved with, was fun. Rooted devices, as close to adrenaline-junkying it up as they could at such an age.

The park was empty. Currently.

Arnold noted that upon his recceing of all the various parks he had scouted out, in and around where they lived, this was the perfect spot to do what he planned on doing.

This park, Goodridge-Park was nocturnally quiet. Peaceful. Today was different.

And all the days Arnold cast his gaze over it, in analysis, piecing together a great scheme. A sting. It seemed perfect. Apt. Today. Even better. Even fucknig better for a paedophile to kidnap his daughter.

When Arnold was around everything seemed to be a place full of dangers and dormant dreads.

Leaden dread, and fear, that could easily be accused of coming from under Arnolds armpits; its hard not to feel that anticipation come over whichever place he was frequenting- like sea-mist. This park had been notorious for gangland related incidents, until the "CHAV-FAQ"-was put into place.

Since all that hoop-lar, it had been reasonably quiet.

For Arnold, too quiet.

Since that had happened, they were on their best behaviour, these gangland youths, as the majority of them couldn't be bothered to be put on the 5-week intensive courses to earn their CHAV-Warrant.

I mean, who would want to be taught slang-words and terms and abbreviations of curse-words and such-like by a Professor of linguistics and one of whom had never set foot on a council estate in their life, and just previewed them on Channel Four and Channel Five documentaries as their basis of analysis and study?

If you had tracksuit bottoms on and there was more than three of you, specifically if you average around the age of being youths or Post-Youths, with caps firmly on, cigarettes and joints exchanged with bops, akin to frenzied starving pigeons, that cocky-I-shit-myself-or-maybe-I-am-turtling-swagger that signals to brain there may be trouble afoot or these kids are just peacocking… and if you're as a gang all huddled together, you were easily assigned, biasedly judgmentally as Gangland Youths.

Or caught lounging, where you're/they're separated enough so they can pose, you're targeted. {Quite rightfully. CHAV-Scum.} as the degenerate youth. The scum of the Earth in motion. Growing up. In front of your unseasoned eyes.

And by certain attitudes, certain perceptions, you are in your own right to confront them, that you could stroll up to them as a concerned citizen for all or potential victims in and around this rowdy bunch of assholes.

Much like a pre-cursor to a citizen's arrest, and all that malarkey and law and given-rule; one could stroll up, *ahem*-ahem, and state "CHAV-QUE-What is your reason of being here?" and by stating as such, you were in the right to knock the little wankers out, if they didn't pull out their registered CHAV-Warrants, for frequenting that select quarantined CHAV only area cum zone.

But after more stabbings, on the Questioners side more so than the actual "innocents" it was abolished.

As was the CHAV-Warranty.

Then, after one great idea from a committee built up of middle-class-they might as well have been upper class- puritans, another took over rather quickly. Another great idea executed wrongly or far too quickly, and apologised for so soon after said implementation. This was the known as The Nonce-Accords.

Arnold had been on a course, relishing the notion that he could catch those "sick-████" out.

And recently this attitude and all these whirling haunting thoughts and the more narcissistic ones, as a whole was swathed into this awful-and-self-crafted notion that a paedo was around or could at any moment knab his child and was in wait for his sweet Cassie. And his concern only for his sweet Cassie. No thought given to all the other kids. Fuck 'em!

As long as it wasn't, or isn't my daughter, I couldn't care less!

All except, he now needs a once to capture his daughter, to enable him to supply his newfound want-of-trade. A Nonce-Hunter.

So he could care less, as far too often he had seen odd jobs around, not in the selected environments he had scouted, but at your shop, watching a man talking ever so oddly to a lone child, one he did not know nor should be talking to, just in wait, almost in hope Arnold was, to reach out and make a grab for it, so he could annihilate the nonce-cunt.

But, that was using innocents as bait, and he just couldn't do that, as he would and could easily be assigned as a nonce and odd- character himself by surveying other children's whereabouts, SO HE JUST KNEW, that his darling daughter, his little girl, his Cassie was his asset.

He grew agitated; obsessed with this fear, and nothing having happened yet, that was where he was left, in total and wholly encapsulated fear, and an extremely illogical fear as most Paedos had either been hunted down or had fizzled out, knowing that there was no chance for them to get up to their Nonce-y ways- so he had no choice, but to use his daughter as bait. His beautiful, kind, sweet, innocent daughter, of whom would come to no harm if he executed and baited the nonce-y fuckers with his ever so delightful and so he assumed appealing young-girl. There for him to catch them, to have the moment experienced, so he could feel a little reassured that this almost urged on event was all that would ever befall her if and when he was around.

Arnold had set up a variety of stings, and many stings in the past few weeks all ended the same way. No Paedo. No interest. No reason for Arnold to kill someone. Yet even to this day, he never had any reason to believe this would happen, the whole Nonce Accords brought on mass and national hysteria by scaremongering, where no one having ever actually seen or witnessed this having happened anyone at all; let alone seen a stranger even go near his daughter, in a perverted fashion or not.

Arnold was growing bored and with that boredom he misread a lot of actions and attitudes and had gotten himself riled up and obsessive, and into a few unnecessary scrapes.

The idea, the fear, being fizzled out by grandeur and delusion, always of fame, of that certain blink and you'll miss it recognition, for what a top bloke he was. Stand up bloke. Hater of Nonce's. And a killer of Nonce's.

Fear. Delusion. Not a good mix, especially about someone potentially knabbing his sweet little Cassie, when there had never been any incident to warrant this strange behaviour. But he felt it, deep inside him, that he had to set up a sting,

To catch one out, not to shoulder off that obsession, that of which he was not aware of having percolating and plaguing his existence,

but to then, after catching such a blatant perv, sicko, that he would be rewarded,

proclaimed a hero, go on The Pride Awards show, for saving his daughter and wiping just one more undesirable and non-entity, and sick-off the face of the Earth: winning out on life, offered many book deals, film rights and all that glorious "stuff!" that he referred to it in his epiphanies...awash with delusion, of fame, fortune and being recognised as a National Hero (that had yet to even happen even to somebody of whom stopped a Paedo a attack, and those who have, had not been recognised for their valour... but Arnold was deluded as well as obsessional).

This park had a certain thing about it.

Odd people coming and going in and around it, in Arnolds mind; anyone he spotted, of whom was either jogging, busy or just a fast walker- he layered his fears and anxieties over them, and just saw potential perverts, to feel the steel of his knife. Arnold had led himself to believe that this park was holding a dormant perv and assumed a wrong-un would frequent this park. Because as one issue was pushed out, or naturally gravitated to a different location, another problem arises.

Even though innocent lives had been lost, all because they didn't fit the right societal bill and description, where they had had been gutted, murdered, beaten tortured all because of this perpetuated fear, where parents rage and fear saw them ploughing them through all the training and the rules imposed and not working within the rules because all they knew was they were legally okayed to kill whomever they assumed was a Nonce.

Innocent lives were lost.

Innocents of whom were scared, indoctrinated by this new Law, that parents were going to prison for doing what they felt was just and right.

All because Billy Bullock had a surname that was a nickname for testicles and had a dodgy lazy eye.

All because Larry Lewisohn dribbled because of too much air escaping through his teeth and collected a canals worth on the inside of his mouth behind his lower lip.

An incident or ten had occurred but after the same shit happening day after day, in the news, headlines steamrolled on out, by old news, new-news, hip-news, rumour-mill news, by gossip, and embellished rumour, it eked out and the usual celebrity puff-piece took precedence, and Arnold like everyone else still looked at someone a bit different with great hostility, and great validated reasonings behind their anger and want to kill, all because this person didn't fit into their biased box of what normal is.

Like the Grass-Sniffer, old Tommy-Bennison, who liked niffing grass, but had no care for anyone else. Bennison was accused of being a perv, but after many confrontations, and Bennison being quite a sprightly man, he luckily managed to evade numerous captures from valiant Vigilantes, or wannabes in Arnolds case.

Arnold hadn't seen him in a while, he had heard he found a job somewhere in Cornwall, centred on horticulture. But he still had a hunch the grass sniffing was all a ruse. *Dirty grass sniffing perv!*

That was the thing with Pedophile's now, the busier it is, the more chance of getting caught, not only that, but ever since the "Nonce-Accords" was put into place, a parent was legally allowed one knife-jab into the suspected paedophile trying to lure a child away, and with a lot of parents, in clusters, at a park we all know most parks are noisy, bustling, and in the old days before this new law was put into place, it was the perfect time for them to launch their kidnapping, but this was no longer the case, on a societal level, as most, if not all, proud-caring-loving parents now, in our day and age, were on constant high alert, possibly higher alert now, because of the new "Nonce"-Accords and the freedom of assumption and biased accusation, that is escalated ever so quickly, before that person in question was given even a fair chance or trial. Courses were held of course for parents, of where to stab, so as not to then get them in trouble if it turned out that this supposed-nonce, wasn't a nonce but just an agitated odd-un of life. But, as mentioned before, this has already occurred on multi-levels in different parts of the UK.

Arnold stiffened, all of a sudden, he caught sight of someone, striding towards his little girl.

Long trench coat. *(PERV!)*

(HIDING A BONER!)

His little girl had fallen over but was already halfway bringing herself up.

NO REASON TO CONTINUE TOWARDS HER, Arnolds thoughts singed. Chimed. He was excited. Time to kill. Still, the trench coated man, with a strangely cocked hat, (made his way*)- IS GOING FOR HER!*

Arnold unsheathed his knife, launched himself, and as he ran, the man reached down, got her around the waist, from behind and attempted to lift her.

He didn't get very far in it, and even though Cassie was giggling, Arnold saw red.

Three stabs to the spine, with a few more dug in, turned, and as the man dropped Cassie, with a thump!-it seemed to go from concrete, up his ankles, to his legs, into his soul, and it made Arnold angrier, manic, crazed, a fucking wild beast- and continued thrusting the blade, in and out.

He heard gargling. Spluttering. A few spat out words that sounded like…"***Arrnnnnn***".

Yes, Arrnnnnn and ahhhhh- all you want you sick perv, Arnolds mind screamed.

And with one final hurrah, Arnold turned, to make sure the pervert would see the face of his…

"HOLY SHIT! *MIKE*?! Oh god…"

"Uncle Mike is bleeding Daddy!" Cassie said, clueless, now sat, soaking up her Uncle Mikes blood, that she splashy-splashed in, giggling. Arnold felt sick, dizzy, nauseous. It all hit him then. He wasn't originally going to set up a sting, he generally was taking Cassie out to see her God-Father, her Uncle Mike.

Before Arnold could let his thoughts catch up, he noticed he was holding a dead weight.

The dead body of his closest friend. Mike.

Who said he would meet Arnold at the park, so they could go get coffee, catch up, and see his God-Daughter....*Noooo, Mike!*

"Fuck!" Mike dropped the body, which farted as he turned to Cassie, smiled, covered in as much claret than she was, still happily splashing in.

Shitshitshitshitshitshitshit!

Shitshitshitshitshitshitshit!

I need to come up with a plan and quick! Arnold had no time to panic. He had to act. His best friend of 25 years was dead as a...

"Uncle Mike keeps farting Daddy, he a stinky dead Troll!"

"Yeah baby, he stinking dead...*Troll*?!"

"Yep. He sleeping dead now hehehe!"

Mike. Dead. Troll. Game. Cassie. Killed. Mike.

"Now baby, take this knife, hold it here, there we go, good girl, now Daddy needs to make sure you're not going to hurt yourself, yes! Yes! Good girl get your DNA all over that...and there...shit, now, Daddy is going to run down there" he indicated down the bicycle path, "I will be back," he resumed, "in a few minutes, and when Daddy gets, CASSIE! STOP! That is dangerous..." Arnold kept patting himself down, looking around. Agitated. Luckily enough no one was around. Arnold plotted out a plan.

A child of three cannot get done for murder. Like that moment in that shit cartoon where a Baby that's yellow and sucks at her dummy all the time, shot that billionaire old tycoon.

Arnold was mapping it all out, what he was going to say, how he was going to construct this.

Just set it up as an accident. Daddy went to go get ice cream, as Daddy ran knife fell out, as Uncle Mike came over, she did, then jumped out and stabbed him, because...shit, shit, think, he must have bent down to pick up one of her toes, wondering where she was, yes that is good Arnold...he must have been panicked, maybe uttered these as his final word as Arnold held him as he died...yes, and Cassie did it because, because, because...FUCK!- Troll...YES-THE GAME! - oh damn she is a child and children shouldn't be anywhere near knives...anyway it will, should, needs to be compelling...but she has...this thing...this thing where she and Uncle Mike play, played, Arnold you killed MIKE! SHUT-UP! Yes, they play a game, they do, they all do, Uncle Mike loved playing Trolls... Knights and Trolls and Princesses and she obviously is always...yes ARNOLD YOU LEG-END!- that was a Game they all partook in and play...shit, now played, past tense and all that shit...SHUT-UP!- so if I can convince little Cass, my little Cass, of this game, maybe Uncle Mike being, no maybe, I need Cass to stab him a few times...as we are, was, no were, SHUTUP!-used to the whole game of pretending to stab Uncle Mike in the back, as he was always the mean troll, never Daddy, always, Unc-Mike-Mike...oh gawd she even created that nickname for him...and upon hearing Mike scream Arnold...that's me... Right...I ran back...and upon, no having ran back...

"Okay Cassie, Daddy needs that, give it, good girl... so Arnold, yep that's me..."

"THAT'S DADDY!" screamed Cassie, flinging up her arms, were drops of blood were sent arcing through the chill 7:58am air Arnold was surprised they hadn't frozen, crystallized and came clattering down as claret-made-rubies... beading his face, a few droplets getting in his left eye...

"Good, girl, good, now stab evil Mike, a few times, good girl, let Daddy help, right there!"

SQUELCH!

"AND THERE! Good girl, this is going to work..."

"Uncle Mike dead? Bad troll dead?"

Yes, well done Cassie, continue with that!

"Yes Cass, that's exactly it, all the Troll game stuff, yes, we're playing...anyway, um, so, Cassie, sweet-pea... let me take that, oh okay, go for it Cass, stab him again, yep, okay...If it feels right do it Cass, stab that PRICK FO A TROLL!- oh, god, Mike...Huh? I feel sick man, that's enough... Daddy will take the knife from you, okay, now Daddy is going to scream, it's a game, as he hugs Uncle Mike...right,ready....steady...*OHGODHELPMYHELP MEEEEEEEMUMUMUMMYMYMYMYMYMYMU MUMUmumumumumummyFRIENDHASBEEN-STABBED!*"

"EVIL TROLL DEAD!" Cassie joined in.

Good   girl   continue   with   that...ugh. Whatthatfuuuughhhh?

"Daddy Troll dead now too!"

Arnold passed out, noticing the hilt of the knife embedded in his chest, around where his heart...

Emptiness

Empty.

Nope.

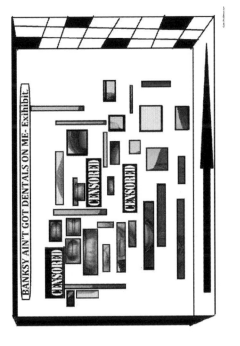

BANKSY AIN'T GOT DENTALS ON ME- Exhibit.

CENSORED

CENSORED

CENSORED

CENSORED

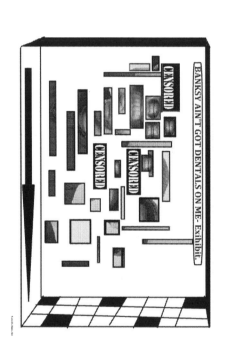

BANKSY AIN'T GOT DENTALS ON ME - Exhibit

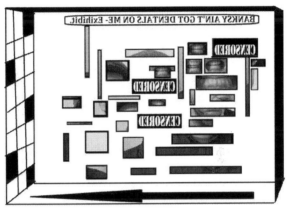

and on and on and on and on and on and on and on
and on and on and on and on and on and on and on
and on and on and on and on and on and on and on
and on and on and on and on and on and on and on
and on and on and on and on and on and on and on
and on and on and on and on and on and on and on
and on and on and on and on and on and on and on
and on and on and on and on and on and on and on
and on and on and on and on and on and on and on
and on and on and on and on and on and on and on
and on and on and on and on and on and on and on
and on and on and on and on and on and on and on
and on and on and on and on and on and on and on
and on and on and on and on and on and on and on
and on and on and on and on and on and on and on
and on and on and on and and on and on and on
and on and on and on and on and on and on and on
and on and on and on and on and on and on and on
and on and on and on and on and on and on and on
and on and on and on and on and on and on and on
and on and on and on and on and on and on and on
and on and on and on and on and on and on and on
and on and on and on and on and on and on and on
and on and on and on and on and on and on and on
and on and on and on and on and on and on and on
and on and on and on and on and on and on and on
and on and on and on and on and on and on and on
and on and on and on and on and on and on and on
and on and on and on and on and on and on and on
and on and on and on and on

and on and on and on and on and on and on and on
and on and on and on and on and on and on and on
and on and on and on and on and on and on and on
and on and on and on and on and on and on and on
and on and on and on and on and on and on and on
and on and on and on and on and on and on and on
and on and on and on and on and on and on and on
and on and on and on and on and on and on and on
and on and on and on and on and on and on and on
and on and on and on and on and on and on and on
and on and on and on and on and on and on and on
and on and on and on and on and on and on and on
and on and on and on and on and on and on and on
and on and on and on and on and on and on and on
and on and on and on and on and on and on and on
and on and on and on and and on and on and on
and on and on and on and on and on and on and on
and on and on and on and on and on and on and on
and on and on and on and on and on and on and on
and on and on and on and on and on and on and on
and on and on and on and on and on and on and on
and on and on and on and on and on and on and on
and on and on and on and on and on and on and on
and on and on and on and on and on and on and on
and on and on and on and on and on and on and on
and on and on and on and on and on and on and on
and on and on and on and on and on and on and on
and on and on and on and on and on and on and on
and on and on and on and on and on and on and on
and on and on and on and on

and on and on and on and on and on
and on and on and on and on and on
and on and on and on and on and on
and on and on and on and on and on
and on and on and on and on and on
and on and on and on and on and on
and on and on and on and on and on
and on and on and on and on and on
and on and on and on and on and on
and on and on and on and on and on
and on and on and on and on and on
and on and on and on and on and on
and on and on and on and on and on
and on and on and on and on and on
and on and on and on and on and on
and on and on and on and on and on
and on and on and on and on and on
and on and on and on and on and on
and on and on and on and on and on
and on and on and on and on and on
and on and on and on and on and on
and on and on and on and on and and
on and on and on and on and on and
on and on and on and on and on and
on and on and on and on and on and
on and on and on and on and on and
on and on and on and on and on and
on and on and on and on and on and
on and on and on and on and on and
on and on and on and on and on and
on and on and on and on and on and
on and on and on and on and on and
on and on and on and on and on and
on and on and on and on and on and

on and on and on and on and
on and on and on and on and
on and on and on and on and
on and on and on and on and
on and on and on...

and on and on and on and on and on
and on and on and on and on and on
and on and on and on and on and on
and on and on and on and on and on
and on and on and on and on and on
and on and on and on and on and on
and on and on and on and on and on
and on and on and on and on and on
and on and on and on and on and on
and on and on and on and on and on
and on and on and on and on and on
and on and on and on and on and on
and on and on and on and on and on
and on and on and on and on and on
and on and on and on and on and on
and on and on and on and on and on
and on and on and on and on and on
and on and on and on and on and on
and on and on and on and on and on
and on and on and on and on and on
and on and on and on and on and on
and on and on and on and on and on
and on and on and on and and on and
on and on and on and on and on and
on and on and on and on and on and
on and on and on and on and on and
on and on and on and on and on and
on and on and on and on and on and
on and on and on and on and on and
on and on and on and on and on and
on and on and on and on and on and
on and on and on and on and on and
on and on and on and on and on and
on and on and on and on andon
and on and on and on and on and on and

on and on and on and on and on and on
and on and on and on and on and on and
on and on and on and on and on and on
and on and on and on and on and on and
on and on and on and on and on and on
and on and on and on and on and on and
on and on and on and on and on and on
and on and on and on and on and on and
on and on and on and on and on and on
and on and on and on and on and on and
on and on and on and on and on and on
and on and on and on and on and on and
on and on and on and on and on and on
and on and on and on and on and on and
on and on and on and on and on and on
and on and on and on and on and on and
on and on and on and on and on and on
and on and on and on and on and on and
on and on and on and on and on and on
and on and on and and on and on and on
and on and on and on and on and on and
on and on and on and on and on and on
and on and on and on and on and on and
on and on and on and on and on and on
and on and on and on and on and on and
on and on and on and on and on and on
and on and on and on and on and on and
on and on and on and on and on and on
and on and on and on and on and on and
on and on and on and on and on and on
and on and on and on and on and on and
on and on and on and on and on and on
and on and on and on and on and on and
on and on and on and on and on and on
and on and on and on and on and on and
on and on and on and on and on and on
and on and on and on and on and on and

on and on and on and on and on and on
and on and on and on and on and on and
on and on and on and on and on and on
and on and on and on and on and on and
on and on and on and on and on and on
and on and on and on and on and on and
on and on and on and on and on and on
and on and on and on and on and on and
on and on and on and on and on and on
and on and on and on and on and on and
on and on and on and on and on and on
and on and on and on and on and on and
on and on and on and on and on and on
and on and on and on and on and on and
on and on and on and on and on and on
and and on and on and on and on and on
and on and on and on and on and on and
on and on and on and on and on and on
and on and on and on and on and on and
on and on and on and on and on and on
and on and on and on and on and on and
on and on and on and on and on and on
and on and on and on and on and on and
on and on and on and on and on and on
and on and on and on and on and on and
on and on and on and on and on and on
and on and on and on and on and on and
on and on and on and on and on and on
on and on and on and on and on and on
and on and on and on and on and on and
on and on and on and on and on and on
and on and on and on and on and on and
on and on and on and on and on and on
and on and on and on and on and on and
on and on and on and on and on and on
and on and on and on and on and on and
on and on and on and on and on and on
and on and on and on and on and on and
on and on and on and on and on and on

and on and on and on and on and on and
on and on and on and on and on and on
and on and on and on and on and on and
on and on and on and on and on and on
and on and on and on and on and on and
on and on and on and on and on and on
and on and on and on and on and on and
on and on and on and on and on and on
and on and on and on and on and on and
on and on and on and on and on and on
and on and on and on and on and on and
on and on and on and on and on and on
and on and on and on and on and on and
on and on and on and on and on and on
and on and on and on and on and on and
on and on and on and on and on and on
and on and on and on and on and on and
on and on and on and on and on and on
and on and on and on and on and on and
on and on and on and on and on and on
and on and on and on and on and on and
and on and on and on and on and on and
on and on and on and on and on and on
and on and on and on and on and on and
on and on and on and on and on and on
and on and on and on and on and on and
on and on and on and on and on and on
and on and on and on and on and on and
on and on and on and on and on and on
and on and on and on and on and on and
on and on and on and on and on and on
and on and on and on and on and on and
on and on and on and on and on and on
and on and on and on and on on and on
and on and on and on and on and on and
on and on and on and on and on and on
and on and on and on and on and on and
on and on and on and on and on and on
and on and on and on and on and on and

on and on and on and on and on and on
and on and on and on and on and on and
on and on and on and on and on and on
and on and on and on and on and on and
on and on and on and on and on and on
and on and on and on and on and on and
on and on and on and and on and on and
on and on and on and on and on and on
and on and on and on and on and on and
on and on and on and on and on and on
and on and on and on and on and on and
on and on and on and on and on and on
and on and on and on and on and on and
on and on and on and on and on and on
and on and on and on and on and on and
on and on and on and on and on and on
and on and on and on and on and on and
on and on and on and on and on and on
and on and on and on and on and on and
on and on and on and on and on and on
and on and on and on and on and on and
on and on and on and on and on and on
and on and on and on and on and on and
on and on and on and on and on and on
and on and on and on and on and on and
on and on and on and on and on and on
and on and on and on and on and on and
on and on and on and on and on and on
and on and on and on and on and on and
on and on and on and on and on and on
and on and on and on and on and on and
on and on and on and on and on and on
and on and on and on and on and on and
on and on and on and on and on and on
and on and and on and on and on and on
and on and on and on and on and on and
on and on and on and on and on and on

and on and on and on and on and on and
on and on and on and on and on and on
and on and on and on and on and on and
on and on and on and on and on and on
and on and on and on and on and on and
on and on and on and on and on and on
and on and on and on and on and on and
on and on and on and on and on and on
and on on and on and on and on and on
and on and on and on and on and on and
on and on and on and on and on and on
and on and on and on and on and on and
on and on and on and on and on and on
and and on and on and on and on and on
and on and on and on and on and on and
on and on and on and on and on and on
and on and on and on and on and on and
on and on and on and on and on and on
and on and on and on and on and on and
on and on and on and on and on and on
and on and on and on and on and on and
on and on and on and on and on and on
and on and on and on and on and on and
on and on and on and on and on and on
and on and on and on and on and on and
on and on and on and on and on and on
and on and on and on and on and on and
on and on and on and on and on and on
and on and on and on and on and on and
on and on and on and on and on and on
and on and on and on and on and on and
on and on and on and on and on and on
and on and on and on and on and on and
on and on and on and on and on and on
and on and on and on and on and and on
and on and on and on and on and on and
on and on and on and on and on and on

and on and on and on and on and on and
on and on and on and on and on and on
and on and on and on and on and on and
on and on and on and on and on and on
and on and on and on and █████████
█████████████ and on and on and on
and on and on and on █████████████
███████████ on and on and on and on
and on and on and on and on and on and
on and on and on and on and on and on
and on and on and on and on and on and
on and on and ███████████████████
██████████████████████████████████
██████████████████████████ d on
and on and on and on and on and on and
on and on and on and on and on and on
and on and on and on and ████████████
██████████████████████████████████
██████████████████████████████████
█████████████████████████ on and on
and on and on and on and on and on and
on and on and on and on and on and on
and on and on and on and on and on and
on and on and on and on and on and on
and on and on and on and on and on and
on and on and on and on and on and on
and on and on and on and on and on and
on and on and on and on and on and on
and on and on and on and on and on and
on and on and on and on and on and on
and and on and on and on and on and on
and on and on and on and on and on and
on and on and on and on and on and on
and on and on and on and on and on and
on and on and on and on and on and on
and on and on and on and on and on and
on and on and on and on and on and on

and on and on and on and on and on and
on and on and on and on and on and on
and on and on and on and on and on and
on and on and on and on and on and on
on and on and on and on and on and on
and oh so fucking on in a continual loop, stream,
chugga-chugga-chugging along. Touch
drugs to slow it all down I do not
touch anything, open my veins, suck me
up, vaporize me, do whatever, inject
me, and you will never need a hit or
puff of snuff of naything else ever
again and then you will feel the goings
on and on and on and on and on and on
and on and on and on and on and on and
on and on and on and on and on and on
and on and on and on and on and on and
on and on and on and on and on and on
and on and on and on and on and on and
on and on and on and on and on and on
and on and on and on and on and on and
on and on and on and on and on and on
and on and on and on

on and on and on and on and
on and on and on and on and on and on
and on and on and on and on and on and
on and on and on and on and on and on
and on and on and on and on and on and
on and on and on and on and on and on
and on and on and on and on and and on
and on and on and on and on and on and
on and on and on and on and on and on

and on and on and on and on and on and
on and on and on and on and on and on
and on and on and on and on and on and
on and on and on and on and on and on
and on and on and on and on and on and
on and on and on and on and on and on
and on and on and on and on and on and
on and on and on and on and on and on
and on and ███████████████████████████
████████████████ and on and on and on
and on and on and on and on and on and
on and on and on and on and on and on
and on and on and on and on and on and
on and on and on and on and on and on
and on and on and on and on and on and
on and on and on and on and on and on
and on and on and on and on and on and
on and on ████████████████████████████
██████████████████████████████████████
████ and on and on and on and on and on
and on and on and on and on and on and
on and on and on and on and on and on
and on and on and on and on and on and
on and on and on and on and on and on
and on and on and on and on and on and
on and on and on and on and on and on
and on and on and on and on and on and
on and on and on and on and on and on
and on and on and on and on and on and
on and ███████████████████████████████
██████████████████████████████ on and on
and on and on and on and on and on and
on and on and on and on and on and on
and on and on and on and on and on and
on and on and on and on and on and on
and on and on and on and on and on and
on and on and on and on and on and on

and on and on and on and on and on and
on and on and on and on and on and on
and on and on and on and on and on and
on and on and on and on and on on and
on and on and on and on and on and on
and on and on and on and on and on and
on and on and on and on and on and on
and on and on and on and on and on and
on and on and on and on and on and on
and on and on and on and on and on and
on and on and on and on and on and on
and on and on and on and on and on and
on and on and on and on and on and on
and on and on and on and on and on and
on and on and on and on and on and on
and on and on and on and on and on and
on and on and on and on and on and on
and on and on and on and on and on and
on and on and on and on and on and on
and on and on and on and on and on and
on and on and on and on and on and on
and on and on and on and on and on and
on and on and on and on and on and on
and on and on and on and on and on and
on and on and on and on and on and on
and on

and on and on and on and on and on and
on and on and on and on and on and on
and on and on and on and on and on and
on and on and on and on and on and on
and on and on and on and on and on and
on and on and on and on and on and on
and on and on and on and on and on and
on and on and on and on and on and on
and on and on and on and on on I
write and here I am trying to capture

my Tream-fresh cream for me-stream team
cream, new and improved where our cows
are somehow vaccinated, teeming,
overfilled. Dream of a stream of
consciousness.

You-have-room-to-process-it-is-all-an-
assault-to-my-mind-and-self-and-
Icannot-balance-it-all-out.-moody.-
angry.-festering in illness and non-
functionality-of-the-the-
productionality-of-the-so-called-
immunity-complex.. an artist asshole
hated unread unloved unapproached
unwanted unread unread no interest art
pretentious obnoxious hyperactive
dickhead words with it their/there
being the issues of ▮▮▮▮▮▮ upon porn
magazines.

Glitter for me…memories negativity and
aching and #painfulandselfperpetuating

#andforeverharmful

#Andselfishlyself-inflicted

Self-inflicted and all that kind of shite and you will have gaps put in-between to illustrate the diversity not even of an autistic persons mind but a general persons mind and thought process and as I write this I am listening to inside of you with Michael Rosenbaum, with Corey Feldman who seems cool but in my opinion, so no slurs, his girlfriend keeps jump-jump-exercise Hollywood-style-jumping, in making me think, is he pussy-whipped?-acting as if she has always been there, woman is interjecting and being far too familiar even in a relationship and as hippie-dippy like as they are together, and as Corey (or is it Korey?) is…still…but she seems to want to partake or maybe it's a strong relationship on their end of things but she seems far too intrusive and all-knowing about him, The Feldster, and experiences, it's all so forced, or wanna wanna wanting to be almost party to his every day of life, like an ego pleaser and I get a sense of golddiggerishness.

Thoughts, conscious streamline coming issuing forth and the only alterations are minor errors…lets backtracked to and highlighted and altered, not that previous one in explanation of the flow I am taking with what is unfolding and being written.

Blank. Interior. Create. Imbue.
Permeate. Drug. Addicts. Hallucinogens.
Sweaty. Enthusiasm. Excitable. Exposé.

BE KIND, ALWAYS.

(Another FB post, where I was trying to educate a few certain people, and knew they would read it, and I hoped they might have felt that shiver of guilt, and changed their attitude, and not so much groveled but showed signs that they were trying to better themselves...Did they? Sure-as fuck-the-did- NOT!)

Treat people how you'd like to be treated. Recently I've come to really sit back and reflect to a point it seems I've summarised this: People are Nasty.

Whether directly or unawares, more thought needs to be given. Need a task done or a favour, don't alienate that person by being sharp, spiteful and self-righteous. Ask with genuine warmth and kindness and understanding. Remember you're asking for a favour. Don't demand. And if that person can't do this or that, never ever then turn it into a sparring match nor argument because for future reference this person will always view a request with back hair fully spiked.
Talk to someone as you'd like to be spoken to.
Especially when you know this person has been down or is currently struggling.

By being blunt, abrasive, sarcastic, self-entitled helps no one involved. Don't continuously break this person down with condescension and childish verbal tactics. Its mental abuse.

It actually escalates, builds, and then the person in question will begin to retreat and ultimately despise you. For good reason. Its bullying. Its mental abuse.

Think about other people's feelings and states of mind, outside of your pettiness. Because that behaviour is, though the person might not admit it, the reason they're down and struggling.

Think. Be kind. Always.

(Okay I will get off my soap-box now.)

I sleep in bed with that soap box, it is so reassuring to know we and soapbox are one and the same. I gave weight, it lends weight, levers me up high to be able to impart weightiness.

PaR<small>T</small> T [h]R*eeeeeeee*

(old) ART-(cyst)Tree.

Papa comes across this act and Daddy sees a perk ass to kick. Sex in a field. Nothing but bean juice and under-age mud-pies with marrowbone and a slobbering dog eye rolling into the back of its head in sexual bean juice ecstasy. Dadda, Papa, of this {insert cliched farm-hand daughter girl character}... Drag across and shove onto the veranda to face Momma's sweet ole' tempered lead.

First he had to fuck and dick' a good lick on her cunt-flecked-clitoris looking dick-dick looking clit-

"FUCK HER YOU LIMP DICK!"

Much to her chagrin she sometimes did fall into that girly mentality, without even being resistant to it and the glances, gleams of hope exchanged between both parents, that never went unnoticed-hoping that:

"This was the day"-

"This is a sign"-

"Our little girl is exhibiting signs of being a little girl"- the almighty sign of their daughter being what their estimation of a young girl should be.

Daughter's innocence retai___.
Hence, we must contain.

It was that/those kinds of looks exchanged that were a wholly accurate summarization that her parents were suffering an obvious grief over not having the type of daughter they strived on having (when having nightly shagathons to the chirps and cheeps and sweet twittering's of insects and ___ bass tones of the snorting of the pigs-lapping up ___it) sixteen years ago. Shaggin' away. 'til the cum ___ s on rumpled sheets. Chisel and hammer to break ___ ___aves.

That look proving that the___ ___re willing that side of her to just break out and take ___ r and stay put. Slut no slut, ala non-slut cluck of t___g___ legs poised, opened luring Papa into her dirty r___. Night dawns. Morning dusks. Duck and cover, there are ducks in here. Quack and quack and quaaaaaarking!

The giggles to become a continual thing, the motions and way she holds herself and the girlish dialogue to spew out of her like nasty cotton candy, regurgitated, for these forms of talks to finally seep in; this obvious resistance to be "the good little girl", to turn into that/their stereotypical/bracket of: ___ *TO BE A NORMAL FEMALE CHILD.* How. . . *TO REPRESENT A MODERN HICK-BILLY SLUT*-daughter.

It wasn't even as if she was deliberately trying to be anything than what she was.

Long dresses never appealing to an alien touch where rippled cloth envelops a child's dead akin... After years of deciphering those looks and their nauseating need to break out that little girl aesthetic, Lesley Anne had taken it upon herself to try and take this unconscious movement even further. ___ vibrate with that sexual rubber-in-outing structure.

Leslie Anne had a daily stroll down the one of the thousands upon thousands upon million to zillions to babazoolions (like her little brother liked to chime...) of land, that her Father owned.

He owned slaves too, hidden in the barn, behind cubes of hay. Cuboids. Huge blockades. Hiding little Chinese children that had been sky-jumped onto his land, monthly, to continue in their fluid, timely work.

Leslie Anne knew that over a trillion billion zillion was where the mark stopped.

Heh! Funny Annie-Boo, she thought, *Be the sweet childish girl Momma and Papa want!*

She broke through a copse of bright corn, some catching on her pointy elbows, scattering around her feet, as the encased leaves came away sharply, as other corn stalks just Boing'd! back in place.

Her Daddy said his farm was very popular due to his Boinging! corn field.

Leslie Anne loved it. As did the local rebels who smoked, finger-blasted their bet mate's asshole to try get a retarded bark to escape their juddering frame,

"SCREAM LIKE LENNY! SCREAM! CUM! SCREAM LIKE LENNIE! LENNY! LEEEEEEENNIEEEEEE-HE WANTED TO PET THE RABBIT GEOOOOOOOORGE! I WANT YOU TO PET THE FOREVER RABBIT...STEIN STEIN-NIGH_NIGH_NIGH_____- YOUFUCKIN'DARE!-you dare shit on my fist Bawb!"

It was endless and held such great secreted avenues...between corn...between corn effected toes...snip at it, tear at it, gosh those *ahhhhh!*- hang-nails are digesting...swallow as baby-daddy nurses a bourbon on the rocks, making the rocks chime and connect with the spherical glass, tinkling...*HARD* stare *CARRIED* over the *LIP* of his whiskey glass...blown glass...classy...unlike his acts delivered unto his daughter... "Swallow them!"- that she could skip and jump rope without anyone witnessing her unusual lady like youthful antics.

Rope that a few prowlers looked at, left coiled, left vacant, envisioning it twined around her pretty delicate throat...if only she could have an Adam's apple issued from below her petite chin, as her legs dangled, as her whole body struggled alongside her dying body...perhaps break on through a materialised adam's apple, to shoot on backwards, within her tubular-frame, known as her neck, to shatter her spine as it pin-balled within that tubular innocent alabaster flesh-streaked neck-venue....

Vast, there for her usage...as future partners pump into her...she was a child...in mind, in certain features...not in height...nor in physical structure...but in soul and mind...Family needs to coerce the age out of her spastic mind... her adventures, hers, and maybe a little bit of her brothers.

It was vastly vast vast vaaaaaaaaaaaaaaaaaaaaaaaaaaaaaaaaaaaaaaaaaaaaaaaa aaaaaaaaaaaaaaaaaaaaaaaaaaaaaaaaaaaaaaaaaaaaaaaaa aaaaaaaaaaaaaaaaaaaaaaaaaaaaaaaaaaaaaaaaaaaaaaaaa aaaaaaaaaaaaaaaaaaaaaaaaaaaaaaaaaaaaaaaaaaaaaaaaa aaaaaaaaaaaaaaaaaaaaaaaaaast. Her brother was younger than her. By twenty years. In her mind...by seven.

Oh and, ". . . very, very profitable", like her Dad often mused, smoke screened by his rolled-up pipe-tobacco-sprinkled into crisp Rizla-smoke, his words much like her Fathers continuous pumping, billowing second hand smoke, that trailed after her in the cool breeze that came from the snowy mountains, north a good fifty-miles off...geography wasn't her greatest suit.

Intermingled. The cacophony of suicidal mountain snow flaked goats heard. Each crunch and collision with the descending ledges and arched curves rebounding, sending the crunch and disintegration of Goat-bone up and into her legs, and ino her vagina.

Sometimes Leslie Anne swore she heard the screams of *"Bahhhhhhh-byeeeeeeeeeeeeeee-biatches!"*- drifting, swathing the surrounding land in radio-waves of Goat-death-bleats, from the mountains peak.

She had happened across a few corpses. One had enough life in it to be aware when she was pinching its Billy-goats tit, pulled, held out in contemplation, in her thumb and fore-finger and eking out the rest of its life and suffering with a nipple-twister, and as she suckled onto its tip, the goat pumped out its cadaver post-death-shit, pouring out like a hose on full blast and decided, Nah I do not want to stop, and its post-death-first-time-Goat & Human-sexual experience-cum-shot, that was forced, strained out, and as the lump ball of twined fur and curdled milk had sprung from its knobbly goaticle it started bouncing a few beats before it picked up enough bounce behind itself, it launched itself to cling to her lower left eye-lid. She pried it off her face, studied it, licked it, felt the strange wet and dried fibres of its grisly fur and curdled cottage-cheese texture and taste, and then spat out a gob of her own internal muck.

Pro-fitter-Balls.

Yummy, Leslie Anne licked her lips ravenously at the thought of such delights to insensate her █████████ ████████████25-year-old cravings... for sugar and cream...slopping   from   a   meat-stick...globules...sometimes   see-through,   with   a mixture of lemonade cloud... and that delicious pastry her Mama' made from virgin whore-trespassers debased, stripped, naturally pored-virginal glandular fever encouraged lard ladled selves...their flesh the lard...their flesh the powder...their flesh the pastry's ultimate intimate element of dominance in the side of 'Merica!

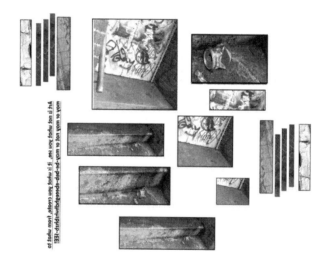

Growing up on a farm, educated at home, socially alienated, cut off from reality...family wanting the best for their dumb-ass donkey sex-humping daughter...though values to those outside of the family ("chugger-chugger-gravy-chain") all pish-pahhed at...flesh not of their own brand and linage meant?- best to manipulate and educate to evolve to add a divined pastry ingredient... from capitalism, from media- the young girl was the personification of living under a rock...as much to the local consensus isn't it the same with all Hilly-Billy-hicksters?- the naivety and innocence of this young-adult-man-child-lady was something one could only reference to the most cliched, in the guts of those awfully bound cutesy in the country-coming-of-age-novels- {found at some middle of the sticks eerie train-station on book-rack, with a rustic tin, painted in spastic handwriting 20C, standing out, superglued to the plated surface- out on a metal arm, awaiting for its first judder of pence to hit the bottom of the tin, to signify that someone would pay Twenty cents for a cheaply bound, terribly written book. If not only to prove the works were profitable but also to jar the entire framework, to reanimate its' inanimate structure, to shed its rustic flakes, to be renewed. No such luck for this non-sentient donation structure. Forever awaiting to be used for what it was for: Donations. And not a back scratcher for the homeless bench dwellers. The tin always remained empty, as passers-by/those waiting for their train/some taking advantage of the long six-seater bench to take rest and shelter under- taking residence for years onward- would either filch a copy or open one up in curiosity and end up launching it out of utter disgust. That and be cloistered, torn, ruffled, bent, manipulated- as stuffing for the homeless, situated under the six-seater bench.}

Leslie Anne was not a modern child, in the least. She was a modern ███████.

She was still a virgin...that her phantom and child-imagined sex-piss-hole... still innocuous and safe. Not from Daddies meat-stick though.

Unlike Rosie Hitchums, who lived on her own farm Westward of her Fathers own, Lesley only knew this from witnessing it herself having strayed a little too far and astray from her Fathers own adjacent land and came across Rosie with ass up in air with a bearded fellow doing something to her from behind, eliciting a crystalline sound from her lips and a squelching from between her spanned out legs.

Only to be revealed to be...tense music...yes, hear it, feel it, we all know it, have a sense of it, what with all the incestuous aesthetic layering itself over the farmland culture and place in history and time and all such notions and potions and sickled pickled gum shoed sextuplets screaming as one has three eyes of its back whilst its siblings possess holes with infectious boils continually bursting...it was her Father.

In the company of them shrouded in corn leaves had been Lesley-Anne's own Mom, with rolling pin between Rosie's agape legs, going in and out and sloshing with powder-puffs and squelching lard bubbled from labia to clitoris to something else that formed her Moms sex-piss-entry-only-zone-yet-here-we-were-squirting-out-liqui-cum-powdered-bakery-ingredients-cement-mixed within her ████-venue.

Leslie Anne continued in her stupor of humming, alternating between dragging along beside her by the bottom hem of her dress, Mrs. Noodles.

Mrs. Noodles was also taken care of by Daddy, and her butt-butt-hole continually sewed up, and stinking of warm sausage filler and the skinned meat, mixed with his lemonade clouded gloop, which crisped up her fur in thick angular spikes that she had grown to love and used as a pick at, to pick at all those spots between her legs, warped on her thighs...

The Doll itself that as a physical thing represented the state of Leslie's mind and attitude to life....the innocence and make-believe reality-those intruding's of abuse and that sad reality will always taint her...resuming into naïve childlike innocence to mask over the real abuse of her life?- **"HOW SHOULD I FUCKING KNOW!"**

A Curse word was a secret thing, far more a secret than making mud pies and collecting them beneath her bed.

Mrs. Noodles' (never having had a Mr. in her life she might as well just be called Noodles, but labels and image and departmentalisation never escapes even the naive and young...even as deluded and ill as they are...solid concrete humps...logic is always fit-within-in-and-around)-hair and her bodily structure and its binding of wool frayed... and specifically cut fur... unravelling as she traipsed along towards the parting in the corn field, lost in her own world.

Spikes collecting cotton drifts. Sunlight streaked through the strange archaic lattice-of its whole rounded wired structure.

Lesley was thinking, as she often found herself to do, thinking, thinking, thinking, she got distracted by a break in an aisle of the long, long, long, endless trodden path of the harvest...

She picked her nose in contemplation and went to eat it, stopping before she could chew it, test its structure in her mouth, finally decided upon to do the most lady like thing, as her Momma absconds reverberated in her tiny innocent little head. "Do not do that Leslie Anne. . .its unladylike, and very un-Hilly-Billy-farmer like!".

-as she massaged oil into the breasts she had neatly lined up in the pantry and the "drying" table, as the ladies of whom were hung on meat hooks were arranged in a strange curtain-styled-fashion and manner to blot out the sunlight making its break through the low-cut-within the hard rock façade of their pantry room-window....and that was to open the left pocket in her floral dress and place it in there for later to add to the growing mass of thick and brownish and green globules and crust balls she had gathered under her younger brother's bed.

The mud-pies were designated to her own bedroom. Sometimes she caught Papa eating them, naked, whilst pissing a pool of nasty murk and moss ejaculates.

She placed it in carefully, ruining part of it. But it did not matter, because so far, a little would still go a long way when it came to her "Upside Down Nose' Volcanico! - that Leslie Anne had taken to call her current project.

It was veering to become something shared as one evening her Papa, Father, Daddy, came in, weeping, as the previous mud-pie was left in a crumbled-on-down (by impressions and ass-clenching) in his open palms, offered in attrition.

"It is the most beautiful use of mud I have ever seen...I only wanted to become one with the mud and land and innocence of brain damaged morphed through delicate hands...oh those hands...no more hands...those hand that have to wrap themselves around my meat stick sadly as consequence of being a retard...I am so sorry...no more hand-stuff my dear...but I need more mud-stuff...pleeease", so she left a few spares, that under her watchful eye ensured was the fore-fronted offerings', the ones she surmised appealed and satiated her Fathers mud-pie kicks.

Leslie Anne had two ways to go in life. Venture further afield in so many ways and grow up or conform to the hick genetics and sensibilities...that she knew was already inherent in the land, in their family unit....or to remain looking from afar like the Hilly-Billy Deluxe Daughter of their side of the Country that she was.

For how long it would remain hidden, unlike her venture with the ███████████ ████████ had yet to be seen or heard or snitched upon by her little sissy of a brother- as Momma hated Dad veering further afield.

Fucking their daughter was one thing, but an esoteric strange sexual need to mate with soil and the lay of the land through which retard fingers made it all into a structure of something far more existential than should be warranted and deemed as what it was, a fucking mud-pie... well that was a wholly other thing, a whole other permit she would not give to her sick-husband.

Leslie often looked at her ████ ████ Timothy and thought it should be him forced to wear a dress and for she to be able to run about in jeans and rolled up shirt, enabled to get dirty and praised for it. Timothy was in his teens.

Timothy wore dresses occasionally, when his Momma wanted to try out a lesbian tryst with a She-boy-son.

Cock tucked into and gaff taped around his groin area and hips to ensure no escape, and place sliced, diced vaginas into her strange egg wicker-basket- made from powdered local girl flesh- that extended, that she claimed was the cunt of her She-boy-son-sex-toy.

Lesley-Anne cast this thought aside and ran for the flattened path. She halted. Thought. Or semi-thought. She went to skip off, when she then decided she wanted went to turn back on herself, something stirred. It captivated her. Not so much too much hyperbole and pointlessness fill in the moist space between her musky chicken feed fed vagina space. She sure hoped it wasn't her Dad. Or Mom. Or that snitch who lived yonder at the next turning. Tale telling on her launching rigid corn on cobs through people's windows.

She paused, feet slowly breaking out, taking a stance, as it did not make her jump or cry out in shock or make her feel in need to head back for home at a quicker pelt. It only encouraged her to track the fast-moving thing down the path.

It was manic in its haste to get away, that much was obvious...it was Adrian...the local normal pervert. Incest was as disgusting to his perverted mind as it was to the real world. Either it was scared or realistically guilty or trespassing and being up to no good, considering she was so far out, and would receive a damned scolding if she screamed to her Father from afar...he only wanted to hear from her if it comes to their Mud-Pie agreement and nothing else...(having already rum out her hall pass for playing Cry Wolf) she decided to take it upon herself to track the thing down.

She was hot on its tail. The mirage, because that was what it was to her, a mixture of rippled silver, projected mirrored imaging that was obviously being reflected off its strange spherical surface- *BULLSHIT*- fanciful delusion...it was the tin-foil hat the perv was wearing, which is best left to go undescribed as to why he wears it and stay on course for this narrative strand...it veered off on into the distance at a great speed. It flattened a new pathway for her to follow it in its furious wake, straying from one acre to another. Corn flew up in the air like rockets, popping and often springing in the force-boomeranging around the air, blurred like UFOs.

UFOS? Screamed Leslie Anne's thoughts. So much opened before her....static...white-noise...terrible signal...

made haste, not

Mrs. Noodles was now left defenseless- discarded, having been snagged by a sharp edge and torn free from Leslie Anne's limp grasp.

to carry her around and have her forced into photos with her and her

apart from those

that were conjured in her mind

settings to pausing,
Leslie Anne skidded, retracting her eager

Anne did

oblivion

precariously pulled herself up
into a striking stance
the contact

holding

ABUTHHHH!

thuffing' 'awwww?!" asked the "alien" pedantically, as
best he

complained...The pervert

This door is not a door, it is a choice. This book is not a book.

It is an experiment. Thud whelp, this safe space, this place place, place is full to the brim with vitriolic errors with unease with obsession with UNRULE with rebelliousness with an attitude problem with no reasoning with all reasoning most of all reasonings with misinterpretation with aloneness comes loneness comes loneliness comes with cum with words with a genealogical spark of union without mush mush mushy mushy moi omit
the moi admit the oi confusion then there might be fusion power cells of cancer drinking a cup of coffee when ology, of ontology,
of cosmetology, meteoric rushes of awards and plaudit and the crashing of shards in slow motion with formational formations where formatting is key and not key where words are written for the sake of defying and defining the sole reason and purpose and ORGASMIC resonance, that there eventually, inevitably

without dissonance and committal of a
full baking sand hut burned to the
ground when STAR WARS fashioned
figurines melt in with your cheap pound
£ store cheap one-dollar store $ where
hype of the hyperkinetic energy and my
favourite thing is Multi-Verses and
potential of crossing overs,
 for nostalgia, for aesthetic, for
expansion, for wide blockbuster variety
of madness and potentiale when words
are words because you fucking make them
and I love my partner and I love how
she is here and patient and
understanding and has ushered in a new
quality to my life that of which is
love. Feel love.
Love them. Love yourself. Love art.
Love the chance to explore and mess
about and not feel constricted by
rules, opinions, judgments, failure is
growth, intended failures is a
subversion of growth in of it-fucking-
self. Hifhlight with pen allf the tpyos
or errors or computer nlegletec
nsegments. Highlight with pen all the
typos or errors or computer neglected
segments. People can easily assign it
to paving over general auterisim and
all such, but I feel there is a beauty,
where we as experimentalist aim to
achieve word-tongue-twisters and also
the unison of mind-melting, typos off-
kilter and truly get under the skin
unlikeany thing I have ever epxienced
and I have experienced this as a reader
myself but even worse as a writer.

People can easily assign it to paving over general amateurism and all such, but I feel there is a beauty, where we as experimentalist aim to achieve word-tongue-twisters and also the unison of mind-melting, where typos off-kilter and truly get under the skin unlike anything we sometimes can achieve, and by editing, we tidy, or extend, I loveto grow ohrt these tnings or just left the tfingers fucknig fly in fury… I have ever experienced, and I have experienced this as a reader myself but even worse as a writer, where we adapt, apply, subtract, re-route, alter, and as experimentalists we strive for a typo, an error, when applied to linear content it truly fucks up with the read and the overall books construction and valour as a piece of physical salable marketable art, and yes it truly does and can get under the skin unlike anything we sometimes can achieve, and by editing, we tidy, or extend, I love to grow out, spread, legs, akimbo, these things or just left the fingers fucking fly in fury… it is art incarnate, born from emotion, and though the typo or error can conflict and overall corrupt a good read or a piece of art or have you guffaw as you may be an uppity snoot-tastic reader, in an experimental book it confuses, slathers on so many imbuements, so many meanings, so many assigned agenda's and purposes, and I have had to put halt on these POD produced books, because of general errors and over sights, that ruin a function, but I look and see that there is beauty in some of those minor, awful, glaring, evident flaws, and it needs to be kept...stretched, warped, built upon, exemplified and experimental innovative and not of the norm functioning pieces of literary realms gives room, and also a weight...no full stops, no alterATIONS BEYOND THOSE KEPT AND LEFT ABD matianed and then objectified. No full stops, no alterations beyond those kept and left and maintained and objectified.

theoretical

or

the young
lady.
    She was your average Farm girl. Rebellious

far away

capacity to birth

a

set to

someone a little older stated

feel

the...

hyperbole

that

what I wish

wish to do with. . ."
"It's in my finger. . .Here

him and he phew'd

that, he

activity   of

A tweak

"O-K!"

unwise- a lot more gun wielding buck toothed mongrels have been let out of their basements since he has had been

so

in those

the masses

probe lengths

in this

put down to an over excited imagination or lack of said imagination."

"Go on" Garl (abbreviation

thoughtfully

admonishments

for her doing so whilst pregnant-

is a spade

T

My

h   a

I am

sa

n

their history books

as a rapist and such being televised/encouraged

the whole planet of Harrumph!

screeched, applauded and

n

exploded with

as

"

"Yes!"

ep

c

aspirations as

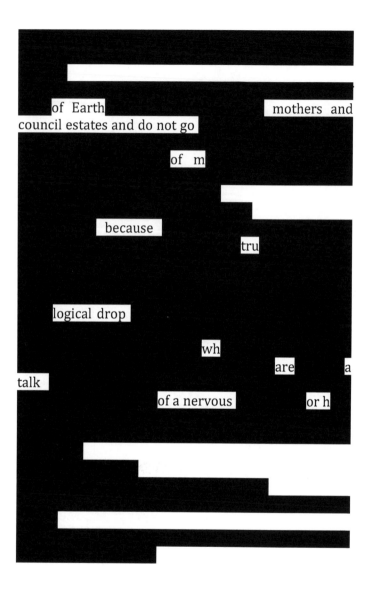

of Earth   mothers and
council estates and do not go

                        of m

                because

                                tru

        logical drop

                        wh

                        are   a

talk

                of a nervous   or h

ely

easy t

sage   as t

r   tt

chatter, screams and yodels had
all seemed to merge into

I   hat

H

IVE   the planning of the
future of their race. Far too excited considering

evolves.

multiple limbs

because it spoils

questioned Garg'

Did you just

Thanks!" she skipped

"Very odd human.

{Interior to a chest of drawers…deep within lies…unanswered love-notes, or un-read love letters, dust, mites, crunchy long dead insects… Or?}

-
<u>A</u>
<u>CRUSTY</u>
<u>SOCK</u>

marks the

That lane, that alley, a short-cut, the comforting wrapping up, like layers of clothing, reassurances, steps faltering, out of complacency and a misguided sense of reality, the reality of a reality of the reality of that geography of motion, psycho-geographically dormant, slim, thine, specific, to reinforce the reality that you may get home sooner rather than later.

That lane, that alley, the end, the peak, the crest-fallen faces of those anticipating something rather specific, walking, coats buttoned/zippered to the throat, hands deeply buried into the pockets. Fibres, crumbs, evidence of past misdemeanors. Images and prose with no relationship, no reason, no purpose, aside from what can be written, imagined. . .

Skips, steps, sashays, jazz-hands motivating jazz-feet, Method-actor elasticity and their beloved pirouettes and fevered steps, where heaviness of steps are falling into the matter of many trod over cement and paving slabs, weight worn, weight rested, weight shifted, emotions heavier than any reusable Sainsbury's (sickly orange) strained, over-loaded bag. Emotions. Mood. Energy. Reserves. Resolves. Intention. Extensions. Words after words. Wet. Puddles. Dirty with scum, wakeful dirt, soil, tarmac broken down and carried forth in the treads of your shoes. Endless, an odyssey into the tangled, angling, arcing, angling, angling, angling, angling, veering pathways, your own personal yellow brick-road.

the end, the peak, the crest-fallen faces of those anticipating something rather specific, walking, coats buttoned/zippered to the throat, hands deeply buried into the pockets. Fibres, crumbs, evidence of past misdemeanors.

Images and prose with no relationship, no reason, no prose-suppose-prose-purpose- aside from what can be written, imagined. . .

Slaps, steps, sashays, jazz-hands motivating jazz-feet, Method-actor elasticity and their beloved pirouettes and fevered steps, where heaviness of steps are falling into the matter of many trod over cement and paving slabs, weight worn, weight rested, weight shifted, emotions heavier than any reusable Sainsbury's (sickly orange) strained, over-loaded bag. Emotions. Mood. Energy. Reserves. Resolves. Intention. Extensions. Words after words. Wet. Puddles. Dirty with scum, wakeful dirt, soil, tarmac broken down and carried forth in the treads of your shoes. Endless, an odyssey into the tangled, angling, arcing, angling, angling, angling, angling, veering pathways, your own personal yellow brick-road.

Fibres, crumbs, evidence of past misdemeanors. Probing, hoping, longing, that there may be a crushed pack of smokes, with a remaining smoke, one you had clumsily crushed with its surrounding shelter- with far stretched fingers, scratching at the packet, in hope a weight sectored in a certain crevice or niche in the packaging may contain a smokable tailor made- maybe it may be a wee bit bent, yet overall, it is smokable, and not corrupted in shape and structure; so that all chemical tar and supposed tobacco flake spills on out, reminiscent of padding put into a wound, in the way it flakes, crumbles, floats, gets stuck, messes up all it comes into contact with… and comes away… with bent smoke, a previously wettened rolling paper, water-dried, now unfolded to save the potentially corrupted, ruined tailor made…*FUCK*! It is all imagination and want…tickle that curlicued R of the embossed Marlborough packaging…cancer…death…port and red meat and 100 cigarettes a day sees a man die aged 93, whereas a health freak dies young and around 21-25 years of age…though is an athlete, and a fitness fanatic…Muscle taut…bound…reboot…entirely built of mean muscle memory and self affliction…dot dash dot sot

Images and prose with no relationship, no reason, no prose-suppose-prose-purpose- aside from what can be written, imagined. . . prose with no relationship, no reason, no prose-suppose-prose-purpose- aside from what can be written, imagined. . .

Canvas-prose with no relationship, no reason, no prose-suppose-prose-purpose- aside from what can be written, imagined. . .

White-Glaring-Purpose-Built-Hollows-To-Create-In…

prose with no relationship, no reason, no prose-suppose-prose-purpose- aside from what can be written, imagined

. . .wistfully smoking, feeling the thick phlegm and lung damage needing a hacking, choking, forceful wet throaty hurl of

"Ach! Eurgh!" prose with no relationship, no reason, no prose-suppose-prose-purpose- aside from what can be written, imagined. . .

praise, ushering in sweet melodies of sweet ego-pleasures, ego-dictates art, without an agonising undiagnosed cancer making its tendrilic, thick way through your flesh-vessel…port…

calling up a call-centre with that free domain piece of digitally corrupted and awfully converted classic piece of muzak…

musk of dirty's…Nazi-Forms saluting to its misuse…

timelines are continually going in, and then the paint-Microsoft software allows childish erasures and alterations and paint drop fillers and icons repeatedly cursed and sworn at…

murky, not as definitive and creator encouraging with all its potential gadgetry and mastery at the click and scrape of a cursor or mouse pad…click, click, click, click, click, click, click, click, click, leading,

to the wall, the hall, the space of personal belief and the images so captured and altered and mangled so as not to get sued, it is all opinion, biased, well-intended, satirical, non-verbal, non-libel, it is all opinion thereof one Zak Ferguson…

THE HALL OF ASSHOLES. More accurately, cunts. Where? Somewhere. In there. An image. Charlton Heston. Gun freak. Amendments ashmendsments. Potato. PoTAR-TOES. Wiggling. Nasty hangnails. Infected big-toe. Korn/ Infection. Immune system is shot!

Evil. Capacity. Capabilities. Accessibility. It is all so wrong. Like knife crimes in the UK. In abundance. People killing people. Kids killing kids. Anger. Psycho-therapy-needed. Locking up. Death chair… The hangmen's noose. Mascara clad goth chicks, not cladded in the way you'd expect…tears, snotty noses, pressed against CHAIN LINK FENCES BORDERING ALL SECURITY lock ups and prisons…containing these semen spurts that should have stayed on the sheets and not impregnated a woman… falling in love with terrorists and murderers because its freaking sexy…freaking hip yawhlll!

but it can still be beautifully subjectively averse to objectivity… Approach as a subjective piece defined by objectivity of its intentionality. Jump a few steps and skip and jump rope and washing dishes for a living hasn't ever been so appealing because this place of work and shit pay has a lead lined bunker and you have your eyes on it for the coming WAR, whether titled WWIII or NUCLEAR. Clear the way so when that awful drone signifies and alerts of the coming apocalypse and then you can leg it, jam it and live. For at least 10 years, waiting for nature to regain its control. Reroute. Rework. Redefine. ReEarth. Population. Humans: 108. Animals: 3 billion. Better hide Humans. Scary. Dish washer aprons marked religiosity.

This is awful just awful, look at the unprofessionalism, the shoddiness, the messiness, the awfulness, the unnecessarily-ness, NESS, the wee
doggie...
....
....
....
....
....
.............semiotics...
....
....
...........the art of the bigger part of so many component
parts..
....
....
.........................so   many
parts..◆.......
....so   many
existential beats...
....heart
beats..sexy thrums and
battering...
...............ram...
.....music.....beats...music...muzak...sheets...........
..........nada....vaccums.........................no drinking on the school premises, unless the booze is shared amongst the teachers room- which is sterile and mank..............momentary youthful ignorance. All they have is nasty mud-like coffee...........stuck in a rhut.........rut...RHUHUTTAH!◆

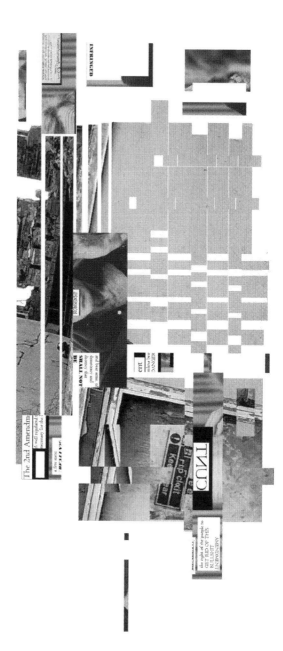

END OF MARK iii
END OF MARK !!!

alright, allright, all right

A{c}knowle{e}dge(*e*)-m{i}ents:

that are not acknowledgments but that are dick sucking-appreciation pieces and prattling's of an experimentalist wanting to share some love and offer out some vague-ish-ish-Billie Eilish-Smith- recognition for a few people and a few presses :

Thank you's go out from this here part. **Thank** you's that are appreciations, dick-sucky moments caught in writerly limbo… and procrastinatory-y-y-recommendation.

So, I am fully acknowledging them as artists, contributors and friends- (that of which I have barely any of).

Firstly, to a handful of people, actually a trio.
Chris, Dav, Paul.

The trio of men of, fine men, mad men, geniuses (*ease up there, you haven't even grasped their metaphorical cock piece yet*)
whom have always been kind, supportive and especially inspiring to me as an artist.

All creative in their own ways that has in so, so, so, so, minute, large, expansive, undefinable and many many many aspects rubbed off on me. Dirty bastards.

Christopher Nosnibor, for his contributions to my podcast, (It's Not a Rant, It's) ARTICULATE WARBLING, an intelligent, wry, dry, rant-tastic man, of whom writes with such passion, such affirmed vitriol at the world around us, that it got me thinking, I like this guy and I especially like hi work. It is fully Nosnibor. And that is a rarity in our overly saturated pocket of the literary universe. He is a talented, intriguing personality and kind individual.

And also, I wish to thank him for writing books such as *THE CHANGING FACE OF CONSUMERISM, The Rage Monologues* and his masterful and extremely Ballardian novel *RETAIL_ISLAND*, that of which is in a lot of ways i an ode, an evolution, a modern-day spiritual follow up to the works of a lot of Ballard's own works- that is so Ballardian that Ballard himself would go, "Fuckin' 'ell! I surely didn't write that did I?" –that instilled in me a new fond appreciation of non-fiction (with *RAGE/CHANGING FACE*) and taught me that satire, post-modernism (with *RETAIL*)* that it hasn't become a satire unto itself, that post-modernism is still what it was or should/would be, that these pieces of fiction and the content and material is still in the Aether, for us to highlight and manipulate, to fit the tone and cadence of narrative and befit the point we so wish to elocute as writers and creators.

---

* Also, the images included in *RI* really goaded me into trying to include some of my own photography, that of which has also impacted in a great way on my current releases and works and seen me grow as a creator, for that I cannot thank Christopher Nosnibor enough- for inspiring me to try my hand at it and it overall working so bleeding well.

Then there were two… ‍‍‍right…left

left…right…where?

The second **massive** shout out goes to Paul Tone, a masterful experimenter with imagery, digital cut-up collage and many other platforms of creation. A writer. A deep thinker. An Educator. A Musician. An Experimenter himself.

A great guy, with a real sense of pride, with a deep rooted- pride and passionate dedication in visual arts, and his music- released under the name *zanntone*; that really sets the mood and also the bar high with **NOISE** music and all forms he alters, adds to and extends off from.

His contribution to myself as an ever-inspired-artist, much like Christopher himself, which were these peoples works, on their own merits, their own terra-firma's of excellence, culminated into something- it was scratching at an itch, their works, their online social media presences, their passion, their intellect, their humour, it was infectious, and I wanted to taste the elixir they were supping and sipping or guzzling upon. What with their standing on vital issues, especially in the UK where all three of us reside (not Dav, he lives somewhere far off in a whole world of his own) it was encouraging, inspirational, with how their art was speaking volumes as well as how they were handling themselves online- it was pushing me towards something. What, I still have no fucking clue. A movement?

Yes! A new movement you could say of crafting, and with it, there was an awakening where a want, a lust to create such gorgeous, harrowing, topical, reverent, Burroughsian-pieces of appreciation, in writing, in collage, in digital means of exploration, with their vistas and plateau of wholly unique imagery (by words and visuals in both their own rights)- it goaded me, inspired me, allowed me to try my own hand at crafting with the visual form myself…

Luckily I got to commission Paul for my Cut-Up/Non-Cut-Up-*Anti*-**Anti**-<u>Novel</u> **DIMENSION WHORES,** which still stands to this day as my favourite cover of all my releases ever put out and in print. A man I wish to work with, again and again.

 Then there was Dav Crabes.
A friend. A strange, mysterious, anonymous entity, one that may or may not be human, who gave me a superb, or maybe not so superb Anti-Introduction for DIMENSION WHORES and has been a confidante, a friend, and a masterful experimenter and writer himself.
   TRAFFICKING and SEXUAL DECEMBER is one of the most purest forms of Burroughsian literature I have ever read, whilst being wholly Dav. He is hilarious, dry, irreverent, supportive, and a writer who needs to get more work on out there, the lazy c*nt!

Thank you also must go out, to the already mentioned (greedy space-hoggers!) Mike Corrao and Grant Maierhofer's, (but, oh they are worth it!) for your dedication to mind-fuckery, to literary pieces of ontological decay and evolution, the reviving of something that never existed...for your combined efforts in fucking with our minds as readers and writers, really redefining something, this vague notion, this vague space, where fellow artists of whom love to mess with form and prose and the interior dimension-scape of a physical and non-physical-meta-textual reality/book-form, for those sublime works that of which there would be no Interiors for ? series...

There are so many others I wish to thank, but this is reading all a bit bum-chummy and sycophantic, but it is what it is, the fucking truth!

I do not wish for this to be something so hyper-so-caffeinated-so-OTT-in my appreciation that it reads as hyperbole and disingenuous, but it isn't. Without these guys and their works, I do not think I would create any longer. It came at such a pivotal moment for me. Not as just an artist but as an individual too.

dick sucking dick
sucking oh so much
dick sucking,
oh so powerful
oh so loving
oh so
so

dick sucking dick
sucking oh so much
dick sucking,
oh so powerful
oh so loving
oh so
so

MAJOR DICK SUCKING ALERT!
fellatio, blowlettio, ball-scrunchio! felt-io!

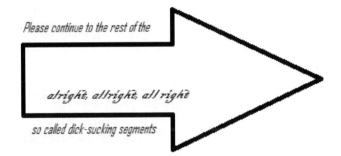

Without the Independent publishers, who specialise in the stuff I love, adore, soak on up and am constantly inspired by there is no art to be put out, emboldened, and championed; without the likes of presses like 11:11 Press, ITC, Schism Press, HEXUS Press and so many more- we are left with the same empty void, where there is no new, difficult, challenging, life-altering fiction put on out there for writers and readers to feel inspired and moved by, to create without any preconception or dictated by the so-called defining rule.

The likes of Gary J. Shipley, (Publisher and Author at Schism Press) and INSIDE THE CASTLE's John Trefrey's are allowing true visionaries, and artists to be read, whilst also being rather ingenious editors, book-makers and writers and experimentalists themselves, to have their work brought, recognised, crafting careers one could only imagine or dream of in the past, and keeping US in the literary verse and adding themselves/ourselves, the experimentalists, the philosophers, the critiques, the poets, the real personifications of creativity to the tapestry of…what?- *something*…something. . .something?!- where we are swimming, percolating, invading the tapestry of time!

John and Gary, and so many others I cannot name at this moment are running amazing, innovative, inspirational, necessary Presses, housing real visionaries, real artists and their works, and those that I have read so far have really liberated me.

I was low, down, and their enthusiasm and passion and pure to the essence and soul of experimentalism, really motivated me to craft as I felt and not as I felt dictated to do.

So, thank you. And to those presses I have yet to experience, or happen across and have so far left out, this space is for you…
I love …{INSERT} {INSCRIBE}   and … this … oh and then there is. . .

Thank you. Thank you thank you thank you.

PHEW! FINALLY. That is over.

Oh, wait, Uno memento whatever and all. . .

Also, I'd like to include a wee thank you to Dennis Cooper for featuring my interview with **scunnard** on his masterful blog, not so long ago, and his enthusiasm for Sweat Drenched Press, something he said, "...feels like a little renaissance or something!" and if that is a mis-quote, god damn am I going to be fucking sued.

SWEAT DRENCHED
PRESS

Please reach out to us
and submit your
(messy, *innovative*, odd, **experimental** wild,
promiscuous)
works
at
<u>sweatdrenchedpress@outlook.com</u>

"Everything is odd, everything is lies, everything is misconstrued, but at least my Grandmama never lied!"-

Old Root-Toot-Twerprehrian

Printed in Poland
by Amazon Fulfillment
Poland Sp. z o.o., Wrocław

55527093R00125